I0538307

The Random Acts of Cupid

WRITTEN BY
Amanda Tru

The Random Acts of Cupid
Copyright © 2012 by Amanda Tru

All rights reserved. No part of this book may be reproduced in any format, either written or electronic, without the express permission of the author or publisher. The only exception is brief quotations in printed reviews.

This novel is a work of fiction. Although places mentioned may be real, the names, characters, details, and events surrounding them are the product of the author's imagination and therefore used fictitiously. Any similarity to actual persons; living or dead, places or events is purely coincidental and beyond the intent of the author or publisher.

All brand names or products mentioned in this book are trademarks, registered trademarks, or trade names and are the sole ownership of the respective holders. Amanda Tru is not associated with any products or brands mentioned in this book.

All scripture references in this book are used from the English Standard Version of the Bible.

Cover design by Samantha Bayarr
Walker Hammond Publishers
Also available in ebook publication.

PRINTED IN THE UNITED STATES OF AMERICA

"But when you give to the needy, do not let your left hand know what your right hand is doing, so that your giving may be in secret. And your Father who sees in secret will reward you."

Matthew 6:3

Prologue

My limbs were weak with shock as I rushed through the hallway, dodging past other students like a fish struggling to swim upstream. I had about thirty seconds to fix my mistake and save my best friend from feeling the worst emotion known to a high school girl—embarrassment.

I could hear my other friend, Britney, struggling to follow my trail.

"Hurry, Elise!" she urged. "Chandra was going to talk to him right after class!"

Tears of frustration burned my eyes. I wanted to snap back at Britney, but I couldn't waste the time. Why hadn't Britney simply told Chandra the truth herself, instead of running to report to me? As much as I wanted to blame Britney, I knew this whole situation was my fault. It had been my idea. I had handled the details. Now my best friend was going to face the consequences.

I hadn't intended on embarrassing her. It had just been a stupid prank. Chandra knew we always pulled practical jokes on each other as birthday gifts." After all, she had been the one to bless me with a brightly wrapped present of lace panties in Art class on my birthday. Now THAT had been embarrassing!

So when I sent her flowers for her birthday and signed the card as Damon Fiest, the boy she currently had a major crush on, I had assumed that she would immediately recognize her birthday practical joke and see the humor in her friends' stunt. After all, Chandra didn't really travel in the same circles as Damon. Since he didn't seem to know that she existed, she should know right away that the real sender could not be him.

No one outside our small circle of friends was supposed to know about the prank. The flowers were supposed to have been delivered in 7th period, at the end of the school day. But before I could find Chandra after school and see her reaction, Britney had rushed up to me, saying that Chandra was looking for Damon to thank him for the flowers!

Dread had sunk like a rock in the pit of my stomach, making me feel ill. Immediate, intense guilt struck me. I panicked. Chandra was crazy about Damon, and now she was going to be humiliated when she tried to thank him for flowers that he never sent! Damon would probably think she was mentally unstable and never want to have anything to do with her.

I felt terrible! What kind of friend was I? Only an awful person would send flowers and lie about who sent them! Why had I been so stupid?

I burst out of the school doors, my eyes frantically searching the grounds. Chandra would have tried to intercept Damon before he reached his car. Since the star football player always parked his old Mustang in the same spot, then Chandra had to be around here somewhere.

Please! I prayed. *Please let me find her before it's too late!*

My eyes tripped over dark hair and a purple jacket halfway hidden by a tree at the corner of the school. I rushed closer, my heart pounding as if I'd just run a race at the Olympics. As I came around the tree, I stopped suddenly, stunned at the scene in front of me. Britney skid to a stop beside me.

I felt my mouth literally fall open in shock as, apparently oblivious to the world around them, Chandra and Damon kissed.

Chapter 1

Ten years later

"Please, Elise!" Britney whispered fiercely. "I don't understand why you won't help me out just this once. This is your specialty!"

Since ignoring her friend was obviously not going to work, Elise turned away from the computer screen and tried to patiently answer Britney without rolling her eyes. "I already told you it doesn't work that way!"

"But you're Cupid!"

"Shh! Elise urged, nervously glancing around the quiet library. "Don't call me that! Someone might hear you. I am *not* Cupid! Just because a campus newspaper wrote a stupid article doesn't make it true!"

"But it is true! Look at how many matches you've made in the past ten years. It's your job; it's your *duty* to make matches. So why not for me?"

Elise wanted to remind Britney that this wasn't the first time she had asked for help, and this wasn't the first time Elise had refused. Instead, she sighed and repeated her standard answer. "Britney, you know I don't make matches for close friends. Part of what makes it work is the fact that the couple doesn't know me well."

"But you set up Chandra and Damon," Britney grumbled. "Now they've been married for like ten years!"

"Six years," Elise corrected, wishing this conversation was over. As a librarian at the University of Washington, she had plenty of work to do. Not to mention that Britney should be working too. Britney should be over at circulation, not "helping" Elise at the Reference desk. Though her friend held a stack of books in her arms, Elise was sure Britney was just using them as an excuse to corner her. "You of all people should know that setting Chandra and Damon up was not intentional."

"That doesn't matter. The point is that you are the reason they got together. You have a gift, Elise." Britney bit her lip and turned her gaze in the direction of the handsome man sitting at a table across the room.

After her inadvertent matchmaking for Chandra and Damon ten years ago, Elise had unobtrusively arranged for a few other couples to "accidentally" fall in love, finding that she had a knack for it. Since then, she had carefully arranged circumstances for numerous couples, people who never realized they were being set up, to find each other.

Britney and Chandra were the only ones who knew about Elise's hobby, and Elise wanted to keep it that way. Unfortunately, she had been so successful at anonymously arranging matches, other people had started to notice as well. It didn't take much to connect the few random stories from around the University of Washington campus about how mysterious events would bring two people together. After the story in the newspaper, the anonymous Cupid was rapidly gaining publicity.

Now Elise felt the pressure of not only the wildly circulating stories, but of the fact that Britney Bowers was one of the two people who knew her secret. Chandra was so busy with her own life, which now included a husband and two adorable children, that she didn't really pay much attention to Elise's projects. Britney, on the other hand, didn't seem to have her own life, and might yet drive Elise crazy! Worse, Britney tended to be impulsive. Elise knew it would be in her best interest to placate Britney if at all possible. Otherwise, there was always the threat of potential disaster if Britney should ever decide to share Elise's secret.

"He's my dream guy," Britney said softly, turning pleading eyes back to Elise. "Won't you please use some of your magic for us?"

As pitiful as Britney sounded, Elise knew she couldn't do this favor for her friend. What Britney didn't realize was that the anonymity of what Elise did was the major reason why she was so successful. The simple facts that the people never realized they were being matched and never connected her involvement gave her the necessary emotional distance to be able to observe people and their relationships without bias. Elise had always been extremely introverted; perhaps because of this, she had always liked to watch people and was pretty good at noticing things that weren't obvious to others.

Elise wasn't going to waste time trying to convince Britney or explain her method of matchmaking. Over the years, Brittney had occasionally tried to get Elise to use her skills in the direction of her current crush, but most of the time,

Britney didn't care what Elise did. However, since the paper had run that article, Britney had developed a renewed interest in Elise's activities, and when Ryan Jenkins had caught Britney's eye, that interest rapidly bordered obsession.

It was too risky to set up her friend. If the match didn't go well, then Britney would end up blaming her. Elise had to be very careful if she wanted to continue being an anonymous cupid. Already the story was becoming almost an urban legend around campus, and the Seattle area in general was starting to take notice.

She couldn't handle the thought of being caught, not to mention that, though her success rate was extremely high, the couples she'd set up over the years might resent that she had meddled in their lives. It was probably better for them to believe they'd been brought together through a little magic. The reality wouldn't be nearly as romantic.

"No, Britney," Elise answered flatly. "I will not set you up." Making sure she had Britney's undivided attention, she looked right into her friend's eyes and repeated in no uncertain terms. "The answer is no."

Intense anger flashed over Britney's face. Without a word, she loudly dropped the books she'd been holding onto the desk, turned, and walked away.

Elise sighed and turned back to her computer. From their looks, to their personalities, to their likes and interests, she and Britney were opposite in so many ways; it was amazing that they were such good friends. Whereas Britney was tall, blonde, and outgoing, Elise was petite with dark brunette hair and an incurably shy personality. Elise had often appreciated that Britney forced Elise out of her comfort zone, challenging her to dance through life instead of always stand in the corner. But at other times, her friend grated on Elise's normally calms nerves.

Despite the fact the Elise felt Britney was wrong, she still didn't like having Britney mad at her. She would have to try to find a different way to make it up to Britney later. As bad as she felt about hurting her friend, she would not match her with Ryan Jenkins. That would be a recipe for disaster, especially since Elise had seen no indication that the man even liked Britney.

After spending the next few minutes trying unsuccessfully to get back to work at her computer, Elise gave up in frustration. She'd always hated to have someone mad at her, and now this situation with Britney was making it impossible to concentrate.

Needing a break, Elise left the computer and picked up the books Britney had left on the desk. She might as well reshelve them since Britney obviously didn't intend to finish the task. She caught the eye of another librarian and signaled that she would be away from the reference desk for a bit. They definitely weren't busy, and if by chance anyone needed help, Elise knew that Sheila would take care of it. The library normally used work-study students to do the reshelving, but sometimes Elise liked to do some of it herself. It often added the variety and mental break she needed during the day.

Elise glanced across the room at the object of Britney's affections. Ryan Jenkins was seated at a table in one of the study areas, focused on his laptop and blissfully ignorant of Britney's devotion. Elise knew very little about Ryan Jenkins, but from what she did know, he was probably way out of her friend's league.

Elise had seen him several times at church but had never actually talked to him. The church they attended was very large and boasted a healthy singles group. Though Elise was very involved and enjoyed the church functions, she preferred to keep to herself and fly under the radar. Besides, from the way the other women drooled over Mr. Jenkins, he didn't need any more female admirers.

Elise did have to admit the attention was understandable; the man was gorgeous. He was tall with black hair and what seemed to be a perpetual tan. Elise had never been close enough to see the color of his eyes, but she had been fortunate enough to see him smile once. Though several yards away, she'd still been blinded by the flash of brilliant white teeth and breathtaking dimples.

Ryan didn't attend the singles functions often enough for Elise to glean a complete profile, but she did know that he worked at the University and was a graduate student. She thought someone had mentioned his field was Law. He certainly looked the part of a lawyer. Whenever Elise had seen him, both at church on Sunday morning and when he came to the library, he was wearing a suit, which of course made him look more dashing, more desirable, and in Elise's mind, more unapproachable.

There was no way she was going to set Britney up with him. Historically, Britney seemed to pick either guys that treated her badly or guys who were quite unattainable. And Ryan Jenkins might be the pinnacle of the unattainable variety.

Drat! Britney had given her Anthropology books. That meant trudging all the way up to the third floor to return them where they belonged. Sometimes Britney's immaturity was maddening! Elise was sure that Britney had known exactly what she was doing when she'd left those books.

As she marched up the grand staircase to the third floor, Elise rehearsed an angry tirade in her head. Not that she would actually ever have the guts to lecture Britney, but her friend really needed some direction in her life that didn't involve chasing after men. It was almost as if Britney kept expecting to meet the right guy who would solve all her problems and carry her off into the sunset.

Elise and Britney had been roommates in college, but whereas Elise had stayed with a field until she'd gotten a Master's degree in Library and Information Science, Britney hadn't taken college seriously and changed her major about five times. Both of them had worked at the library while students, and when Elise got her graduate degree, she was hired as a Research Librarian and Information Services Coordinator. Elise had done well in her position, and her duties now included other responsibilities. The rumor was that Elise would be promoted into her boss's position when he retired in a couple years.

Britney, on the other hand, had stayed in the same minimum wage library assistant position that she'd had in college. She hadn't graduated with a degree, yet she still took random classes with no clear purpose. It almost seemed as if she was stuck. She didn't know what she wanted out of life and was seemingly content to spend her parents' money while she waited for that Prince Charming to come rescue her.

Britney occasionally went to church with Elise, but she could definitely not be said to be dedicated to her faith or her church. In fact, Elise often suspected Britney only came to church to check out the male selection. Seeing Ryan Jenkins at church had only intensified Britney's crush on him. After all, she had been scoping him out at the library for months.

Though Mr. Jenkins came in fairly frequently, Elise had never seen any evidence that he liked or was attracted to Britney in any way. Elise would often cringe as she witnessed her friend find some excuse to interrupt the man's studies or find ways to "help" him. Mr. Jenkins never approached Britney or instigated a conversation, but he always seemed polite and not overly bothered by Britney's antics. However, Elise still hadn't seen that spark of interest that would indicate he thought of her as more than just a library employee.

Heading toward the bookshelves, her eyes caught on a group of people occupying one of the study rooms. The window along the front allowed her to easily see the students seated around the table. As she checked the numbers and carefully slid the books alongside their siblings on the shelf, she was also able to unobtrusively watch their study session.

This particular group of six students had been meeting regularly this semester, studying for their upper division history class. Though Elise familiar to Elise, she couldn't say that she really knew anyone in the group. But she actually knew plenty about them. After all, this wasn't the first time she'd spied on them, though Elise really disliked the term "spying." She was closely observing with the motive to help. That really couldn't be termed "spying," right?

With satisfaction, she saw the girl with long brunette hair, Shelby, steal a glance at the blond guy, Clay. Then, about a minute later, she saw Clay's eyes light up when Shelby said something.

Now she knew for sure that she'd been right. Those two *did* like each other!

Elise had watched them interact for weeks. The furtive glances and smiles passed between them had made her suspicious. With a few more observations and well-worded questions when each of them had come for help, she'd learned their names and gathered that each of them was single and more than a little shy. Clay didn't seem to realize that Shelby was just as attracted to him as he was to her, and vice versa.

Elise put the last book on the shelf with a smile. It was time to put her plan in motion. If she could arrange for Clay and Shelby to have an "accidental" date, she was sure they would be able to overcome their reserve and make a connection. She'd had her eye on the two of them for a while. Valentine's Day was in just a couple of days. If everything went according to plan, Clay and Shelby would be a couple by February 14th.

As she went back down the stairs and returned to the Reference desk, Elise saw Oliver Purdue trying to talk to Britney. Elise smiled in amusement as Oliver followed Britney around the staff area like a puppy dog. Oliver was another library employee and also happened to be hopelessly enamored with Britney. He'd had a crush on her since he started working at the library about a year ago. Elise felt sorry for him. He really was a nice guy, and Elise wished Britney would give him a chance.

But even though Britney knew he liked her, she found him intolerably annoying. Also unforgivable to Britney was the fact that he was about two years younger than her and looked the part of a typical nerd. He wore glasses, was always a bit over-dressed for work, and had a great fondness for computers.

Elise had tried to tell Britney how nice and thoughtful Oliver was, but Britney had no desire to look beyond the stereotype. Instead, Britney was frequently rude and condescending to the poor man, and yet, to Elise's amazement, he cheerfully kept trying to earn Britney's favor.

Attempting to focus on the report she was working on, Elise tried to mentally push all the people and problems aside. Five minutes later, she had succeeded in burying her mind to all but the words in front of her.

"Excuse me."

Elise startled, literally jumping several inches off her chair at the sound of a deep, unexpected voice. Turning, she found the tall, gorgeous Ryan Jenkins standing at her desk.

Chapter 2

Her shocked brain immediately registered the fact that his eyes were hazel—an unusual, heart-quickening shade between brown and green. And then she realized those beautiful eyes had lit with amusement—at her.

Trying to gracefully cover her ridiculous reaction, Elise rose from her seat. She really should remember not to get so engrossed in her work. She was, after all, a Research Librarian. Part of her duties was to help those needing assistance with research-related questions. She tended to let the quiet calm of the library make her a little too oblivious at times.

"What can I help you with," Elise asked smoothly, trying to figure out what to do with her hands and their sudden urge to fidget.

"It's Elise, right?" he asked. "Or maybe I should say Miss Hutchins? I remember seeing you at church."

He remembered her! No one ever remembered her from anywhere! Most of the people she graduated high school with had never even realized her existence.

"Elise is fine," she said simply. "And you're Mr. Jenkins, correct?"

"Ryan," he replied. Then, apparently satisfied with the pleasantries, he continued. "I had ordered a book from another library. Would you mind checking to see if it's in route? I thought it would be here by now."

"Oh, sure." Elise took his University ID and typed the information into her computer. Out of the corner of her eye, she glimpsed Clay passing by on his way to the doors. As he caught her eye and raised his hand in his customary friendly wave, Elise stopped him, signaling for him to come to the desk.

"I have that group study room scheduled for you tomorrow as well, is that correct?"

"I guess," Clay replied. "If Donovan scheduled it, then I'll be here. Same time?"

"Yes, that's what is scheduled."

"I guess I should always check with you before leaving, Miss Hutchins. Donovan's great at scheduling the study sessions, but not so good about letting all of us know. We were supposed to have two other people tonight, but he forgot to invite them."

"I don't think that's the first time your group has had missing members," Elise said with a smile. "Don't be afraid to ask. You can talk about it with the others, but I can also set up a reminder email to let all of you know when your study session is scheduled. That might be easier than depending on someone else for information. And remember to just call me Elise."

"Okay, thanks. That sounds like a great idea. I'll let you know."

Feeling a bit guilty about the interruption, Elise returned to her computer, an apology to Ryan on her lips.

She frowned. "It's showing that your book was sent several days ago. We should have already received it. You didn't receive an email notice that it had arrived?"

"No. I didn't. I guess I should have just gone to the other library and picked it up myself. It's on campus. I just thought it would save me a trip since I usually come here."

Then she saw Shelby from Clay's group study session slide up behind Ryan, as if in line.

"Did you need something, Shelby?" Elise asked, not stopping to think about how rude she may be appearing to Ryan.

Shelby moved forward shyly and slid a book onto the counter. "This is the book you recommended, Elise. I just wanted to let you know how much I enjoyed it. You were right, it was a great book. Thanks."

"You're welcome! I'm so glad you liked it. I know you're busy right now, but maybe before Spring break, we can talk and I can load you down with some more of my favorites."

"I'd like that," Shelby said with a smile.

"Oh, and while you're here, I should probably remind you that I have your group on the schedule for tomorrow afternoon at 4:00."

"Okay, thanks. I'll see you then."

Looking back at Ryan, she suddenly realized how rude she'd been. "I'm so sorry, Mr. Jenkins! I wasn't... I don't normally... I... I'm sorry!" Elise's humiliation only got worse as she fumbled for words.

"Don't worry about it," Ryan replied with a gentle smile. "No harm done. I'm not in a hurry. But I will be upset if you continue to call me Mr. Jenkins."

Elise's mouth curved in a shy smile before ducking her head back down to the computer. About thirty seconds later, she realized she needed to make another apology. "I'm sorry. Ryan. I don't know where your book is. I'll call the other library to make sure it was sent, and then I'll try to trace where it got lost. It might have arrived here but been misplaced. If you check back with me tomorrow, I'll have some news for you."

She slid one of her cards across the counter. "If you call me, I might be able to save you the trip of coming in. I'll be working until 5:00 tomorrow."

"I'll probably be in tomorrow anyway," he said, even as he took the card and put it in his wallet. "I certainly hope it shows up. I really need it for the research I'm doing."

Elise wanted to ask him what he was researching. That, along with about twenty other questions, waited for her lips to speak and let them loose, but she remained silent. Ryan Jenkins wasn't looking to start a conversation with her; he was looking for his book. He would think she was way too nosey if she started asking questions. So she kept her mouth shut and just nodded. She'd learned long ago that there was less chance of embarrassment or pain if she stayed quiet. She liked to observe people, just not interact with them.

"Thanks for your help," Ryan said, picking up the carrying case that held his laptop. After all, she hadn't offered him a reason to stay and talk. "I'll probably see you tomorrow. Oh, can you check these two books out for me here? Or should I go to the other desk?"

"I can check them out for you," Elise replied, taking the two books. She saw that both were related to Law topics. As she scanned the codes on the books, she glanced nervously across the room. She should have probably made Ryan check the books out at the circulation desk. Britney would have been the one to assist him. If Britney saw Elise helping Ryan, she might get even more upset.

But thankfully, Britney wasn't looking her direction. In fact, she was still very conveniently distracted by Oliver. It looked as if he was trying to show Britney something on the computer, but even from across the room, Elise could feel Britney's frustration and see the angry glares she sent Oliver's way.

"Thanks, Elise, I'll see you tomorrow." With a smile, Ryan turned and walked to the doors.

Elise sat back down at the computer. What could have happened to that book? She flipped over to her email account. Maybe she'd send a librarian at the other facility a message and see if she could check things out from her end.

As she brought up her email, she saw she had a message from Britney. Elise clicked on it.

I'm sorry I got so upset. I know I shouldn't depend on you to fix my life. I just have this feeling that Ryan and I are meant to be together, and I don't know what to do about it.

Elise smiled. Britney had no problem walking across the room to make her request earlier, but she sent an email to apologize. At least it was an apology. Elise would take it. Britney was always quick to get upset, but she was also quick to make things right. That's probably why they had stayed friends for so long. It also helped that Elise was never one to hold grudges.

Elise sent her email to the other librarian and looked across the room to find Britney. She wanted to let her know in person that all was forgiven. Elise felt her mouth open in shock. Ryan had never made it out the door. Instead, he was talking with Britney near the circulation desk. Having apparently ditched Oliver somewhere, Britney was smiling flirtatiously up at Ryan, every syllable of her body language shouting that she adored him. But Ryan himself was most surprising. He was smiling back at Britney and nodding as if enjoying the conversation.

Maybe Elise had been wrong. Maybe the two of them being together wasn't so far-fetched after all. Maybe Ryan actually *was* attracted to Britney. Maybe... just maybe... But should Cupid do something about it?

Chapter 3

"I'm not going to make it tonight, Elise."

Elise felt the stab of disappointment at Chandra's words. She'd been looking forward to seeing the show with her friend.

"Joey is sick, and I can't leave him," Chandra continued.

"I understand," Elise replied, trying to instill enough cheer in her voice so that Chandra wouldn't be able to hear her disappointment over the phone. Chandra's voice sounded tired and stressed as it was. Elise didn't want to add to her friend's worries. "That's okay."

"I'm sure you can get someone else to go with you. What about Brit—"

"You know she hates these things. Remember when I first got the tickets? I asked if she wanted to go with us, and she said she was busy that night washing her hair. And that was before she even knew the date."

"Well, I'm sure someone else will go with you," Chandra urged. "Those are really good tickets. You should ask around."

"Sure. I'll figure something out," Elise replied, purposely noncommittal.

"You're not going to ask around, are you." It was a statement. Chandra knew her very well.

Elise was silent.

"Come on, Elise. I know you're an introvert, but that's no excuse for going to a Broadway show *alone!*"

"I'll be fine, Chandra. Don't worry about it."

Chandra let out an exasperated sigh.

Elise wished she had the guts to ask someone to go with her, but the mere thought of approaching someone about it was just about enough to send her into a panic attack. What if that someone said no? Worse, what if he or she said yes? Then Elise would have the stress of trying to be personable for an entire evening. No, Chandra was safe. If Elise couldn't go with her friend, then she'd rather not go with anyone at all.

"Oh, gotta go!"

And Chandra hung up before Elise could respond. Joey was probably getting sick again. Poor little guy! Poor Chandra!

Elise was much too busy to waste time worrying about something she couldn't change. She had to finish work here at the library, then get busy with all her plans. It would have been nice to share some of those plans with Chandra, but she couldn't let that stop her. Too many people depended on her actions in the next 36 hours or so. After all, tomorrow was Valentine's Day.

Trying to finish the project she was working on, Elise focused on her computer. She had to leave in about 30 minutes and needed to get as much done as possible before then. She'd really jam-packed her schedule this year. She really hoped the timing on everything would work out.

"Excuse me, Miss Hutchins, may I have a word with you?"

Elise startled, but not so much because of the interruption as due to the sharp tone of voice. Her gaze swung to find Ryan Jenkins once again standing at the Reference Desk. Shocked and confused at the anger she found seething in his eyes, Elise jumped up and grasped at the only explanation she could think of.

"I found your book!" she said excitedly, holding the heavy book out to him across the counter.

Ryan didn't even glance down at the book, but instead kept his intense gaze steady on Elise.

"Can I please have a word with you in private?" he gritted out.

"Of course," Elise replied, not sure what he had in mind. She looked around nervously. They couldn't really get more private than they already were. It was a library, and it was only sparsely populated at the moment.

"Can you take a break?" Ryan asked.

"Sure," Elise replied, understanding that he wanted her to follow him. She always worked more hours than required by contract, and she rarely took breaks. Knowing she wouldn't be able to focus anyway, she abruptly decided to leaver her to-do list for another day and take off work a little early. She quickly grabbed her coat and purse and came around the counter. "Just let me tell Sheila."

At the circulation desk, Sheila flashed Elise a strange look at the announcement that she would be taking off early. Elise smiled, trying to dispel any of her coworker's concern or curiosity over the fact that this was probably the first time ever Elise had "taken off early."

Elise's smile fumbled as she met Ryan's hard gaze again. Why was he mad at her? He hadn't even taken the book she'd found for him. He'd left it at the Reference Desk. Not that she'd ever admit it to him, but she'd gone to a lot of work to locate it. After being unsuccessful with her emails and phone calls, Elise had personally gone to the other library this morning before reporting for work. Another librarian had assisted Elise in her fruitless search. Finally, they'd discovered that the book had never been sent but had been displaced after being checked off as sent. Almost 45 minutes after setting foot in the building, Elise had left to return to her own library, Ryan's book securely in hand.

Now it looked like all of her work had been wasted. Not only did he no longer want the book, but he obviously hated her. And she had no idea why. What had changed since yesterday?

Elise followed Ryan out the front doors of the library. Not surprisingly, it was raining outside. Frequent rain was part of life in Seattle. It was the necessary part of keeping the Emerald City green. Instead of walking down the steps into the rain, Ryan moved to the side, staying close to the building under the protection of the elaborate, overhanging roof. The library and its beautiful architecture was one of the landmarks of the campus. Coming out the door of the huge building with its tall arches and looking across the wide brick commons area they called Red Square, always made Elise feel small. Now it just succeeded in making her feel even more intimidated than she already felt.

Ryan turned to face her, pinning her with fierce eyes that, at the moment, looked more green than brown. Elise immediately understood how he could be successful in the field of law. She already felt guilty under his scrutiny, and she had no idea what she'd even done.

Ryan leaned close, his words clipped in anger. "Would you mind telling me, Miss Hutchins, why your friend, Britney Bowers, approached me earlier and profusely thanked me for the flowers I sent to her?"

Elise fumbled, "I'm not sure… I think Britney worked earlier, but that was before my shift started. I'm only working from noon to 5:00 today."

"I'm well aware of when Britney was working. I came to the library this morning where she accosted me with her appreciation over the big bouquet of a dozen red roses sitting on her desk."

"Maybe she misunderstood… ?"

"She showed me the card that came with the flowers. I just happen to have it with me." Out of the pocket of his suit, he pulled a card out and handed it to Elise. It was from a florist—the florist Elise always used. Ryan thrust the card into Elise's shaking hands. It read, *Here's to possibilities, Love Ryan Jenkins.*

Elise opened and closed her mouth, completely speechless. She didn't know how to respond. This was bad. This was very, very bad.

And then it got worse.

"I didn't send the flowers," Ryan reiterated. "But I know *you* did. I told Britney straight out that they were not from me. She seemed very upset and disappeared into the staff area. I took the card and went directly to the florist to find out who had made the purchase."

"Why would they tell you?" Elise asked in confusion. "I thought that kind of thing was confidential."

"Oh, it probably is. But I'm a lawyer. I can be very persuasive. And when persuasion fails, I can be downright intimidating. I told them I did not send the flowers, and I strongly *suggested* they tell me who had used my name to commit fraud."

"And they told you…"

"Your name. You had called. You had placed the order. They even showed me the invoice with your name and your credit card."

Elise felt sick. She didn't know what to say. She was shocked. She was embarrassed. She was afraid. Feeling the burn of tears behind her eyes, she looked away from Ryan, trying to feign sudden interest in the few umbrellas bobbing across Red Square.

"I'm sorry," she said softly, fully knowing the words were far too inadequate. But she wasn't willing to offer an explanation. She knew it wouldn't do any good anyway.

"Sorry isn't quite good enough, Miss Hutchins."

"Elise," she correctly quietly.

"*Miss Hutchins*, look at me!"

Not knowing what else to do, Elise quickly acquiesced and swung her gaze back to him, but she avoided his eyes. She couldn't take those beautiful eyes looking at her with such disgust.

"I have a theory. Let me explain it, and you tell me if I'm right." Not waiting for her response, he continued. "You see, I don't think this is an isolated incident. A campus newspaper ran an interesting story a few weeks back. Did you happen to read it?"

Once again, he didn't seem to need a response from her.

"I think you're Cupid."

Chapter 4

At that moment, Elise understood what it meant to have your blood run cold.

"Or maybe I should say, I *know* you're Cupid," Ryan said with conviction. "I reread the article and did a little investigating. It seems a little strange that a large percentage of the couples matched by Cupid work at or frequent the library."

Elise shrugged. "It's the University library. Of course everyone comes here."

"But do a lot of them also frequent your church?"

Elise made the mistake of looking into Ryan's eyes. He was a well-trained lawyer, and she was being interrogated. The second she made eye contact, she realized he could see the truth and her sense of guilt. There was no use denying it or trying to pretend that his theory was far-fetched.

"You were trying to set me up with Britney Bowers, weren't you?

"She is crazy about you, Ryan!"

"But I am *not* crazy about her! There is no excuse for you sending her flowers and pretending they were from me. That's deception and borderline fraud! And you claim to be a Christian! How can you justify your behavior? You interfere in others' lives without permission. You are dishonest. You lie and deceive. Why? Does the end justify the means? My first impression of you was that you were a shy, sweet, Godly woman of good character. I can't believe I was so wrong."

Elise shook her head, tears making trails down her face. She somehow knew it would do no good to defend herself. He had completely misunderstood and misjudged her. But she didn't have to stand here and listen to him rant and lecture her.

"Obviously nothing I say is going to change your opinion of me, so if you're done..." Elise turned and fled down the steps and into the rain, her feet flying across the wet bricks.

Suddenly, Ryan was in front of her, blocking her path across Red Square.

"No, I am not done!"

In their haste, neither one of them had bothered with an umbrella or even a hood. Elise looked up at Ryan, frustrated, yet still almost mesmerized at the droplets of water dampening his hair and trickling down the angular planes of his face.

"What you are doing is wrong!" Ryan said, his features clothed with an intensity that only enhanced his rugged good looks. "Does anyone else know about how you like to toy with others' lives? You're famous now since that article. I think you deserve to enjoy your popularity. So I'm going to help you out with that. I intend to inform the newspaper of Cupid's identity. I also think your supervisor at the library will find it very interesting to know how you're using your position to "help" others."

Elise was horrified. With her hand covering her mouth, she just stared at the wickedly handsome man in front of her.

"Please, Ryan. Please… don't tell." Her mind went to all of the couples she'd matched. How would they feel when the magic and romance of an anonymous Cupid was suddenly brought into the realm of reality? What would her boss say? Would everyone misjudge her as severely as Ryan? She didn't think she could handle the shame and embarrassment.

At her plea, Ryan's expression didn't relent even a little. "It's the right thing to do. What you do is unethical, and this is the only way to have all the secrets out in the open. You made your choices, and now you have to deal with the consequences."

Elise closed her eyes, her throat constricting in pain from trying to keep the tears from joining the rain that coursed down her hair and face. She longed to set things right! Ryan had misunderstood everything, and yet she doubted he would listen to an explanation, even if she could give it. He had positioned himself as judge and had convicted her without a trial. Now he was handing down her sentence. And it was harsh.

Elise felt a strange mixture of shame, anger, and sheer panic. What kind of lawyer was he? She deserved a good defense, or at least the chance of a trial. If only she could offer a case that he would understand and accept.

That's when a sudden, ridiculous idea hit her.

"Okay," she said.

"Okay, what?" Ryan asked, obviously suspicious over her abrupt mood change.

"Okay, you can reveal my identity. But before you do so, I have a request."

"What?" His suspicions were not appeased in the least.

"Give me twenty-four hours."

"How is twenty-four hours going to help?"

"I want to present my case," Elise answered firmly. "You have made assumptions that aren't true and judged my character in the worst possible light. You are wrong about me, and I would like to have a defense."

"What exactly did you have in mind?" While not open, his expression was at least curious.

"Are you busy tomorrow? I know you won't believe me if I just tell you what I do and how your opinion of me is wrong. You don't know me at all, so I need to show you who I am. You need to observe what I do to match couples and why I do it. If at the end of twenty-four hours, you still want to broadcast my story, go ahead. I won't stop you, and I won't deny that I'm the Cupid the paper was talking about."

Ryan stared at her for a full ten seconds. She could feel the rain soaking her hair. A few droplets escaped down her neck, trickling down her back and sending reflex shivers throughout her body. But she maintained eye contact with Ryan, refusing to even blink.

"Okay," he said. "I'll give you twenty-four hours. But I'm not available tomorrow morning. I have to teach a class and then go home for a conference call."

"That's fine," Elise said quickly, relieved and yet a little scared he'd change his mind. "I have shopping to do tomorrow morning anyway. We'll make it work."

Elise looked at her watch. "Come on. Let's go."

Elise took off at a brisk pace back across Red Square and up the steps to the library.

"Wait a minute," Ryan said, at her elbow as they once again reached shelter from the rain. "Where are we going?"

Not stopping, Elise continued to the library doors. "You agreed to follow me around for twenty-four hours, right? Well, my defense starts right now."

Chapter 5

Ryan's surprise visit and the resulting drama had caused her to completely forget the appointment she had scheduled. She hoped she wasn't too late.

Elise led the way up the grand staircase to the third floor.

As she walked past the glass-windowed group study rooms, she quickly saw the objects of her mission. Continuing past the room, she ducked behind a bookcase that provided a perfect line of sight.

"What exactly are we doing here, Miss Hutchins?" Ryan demanded, not bothering to follow Elise's lead with concealing himself and not caring to use a library whisper.

He was going to ruin everything!

"Shh!" Elise said, putting one finger to her lips in a silencing gesture and using the other hand to grab Ryan's and pull him back behind her.

Shocked at her own boldness, Elise quickly released Ryan's hand as if it had thorns and turned to explain. Facing his angry expression, her fierce courage suddenly abandoned her.

"Exhibit A," she said, simply pointing to Group Study Room 2.

Ryan obediently peered around the end of the bookcase. "Aren't those the same students you were talking to yesterday about their group study session?"

"Yes. Clay and Shelby." Elise paused, nervous about how Ryan would react to her explanation. She'd never actually had to explain her matchmaking scenarios to anyone. Chandra and Britney had come along a couple times, but at this point, they almost took Elise's unusual hobby as a matter of course.

"But aren't there supposed to be more students in the study group?" Ryan asked, clearly impatient but trying to play along. "They are the only ones in there."

Finally, she took a deep breath and dove in. "I set them up. I've known for months now that they really like each other. But Shelby is very shy, and

Clay is somewhat of a nerd. Clay didn't seem to think that a beautiful girl like Shelby would ever be interested in him."

"So you told them there was a study group session today when there actually wasn't," Ryan filled in.

"Not exactly," Elise hedged, well-aware of his disapproving tone. "I just told them I had the study room scheduled. They usually have study sessions on this day, but their leader didn't schedule it for today. So I scheduled the room myself; I just didn't tell them they would be the only members in attendance."

"That's still a lie, Miss Hutchins. Whether you told them something that was untrue or you led them to believe it, you're still being deceptive."

Elise felt a jolt of fear. Maybe he was right. She tried so hard to make her matches in ways to wouldn't compromise her faith or ethics, but maybe she was wrong to do any of it.

"Ryan, would you please reserve your judgment of me for twenty-four hours?" Elise asked calmly and quietly. "Then I give you permission to rant and rave and lecture me all you want."

"Fine." Ryan replied, though his tone suggested his attitude about their arrangement was anything but fine. "But you can't exactly expect me to be a silent observer."

"Of course I don't. You can talk or ask whatever questions you like. I would just prefer to postpone questioning my character and labeling me a liar until you really know me."

Ryan's brooding silence was his only response.

"Look at them, Ryan," Elise urged, as she moved over a few inches so he could see past the end of the bookcase to the window of the study room.

Ryan moved closer, his arm brushing hers.

Elise spoke softly. "Do you think they really care that they were set up and the rest of the group isn't going to be here?"

It looked as if Clay and Shelby had completely forgotten they were supposed to be studying. But even from a distance, the smiles on their faces were obvious. Clay looked as if he'd just found out he was heir to a fortune, and the soft glow on Shelby's face was reminiscent of what Snow White must have looked like when first awakened to find her prince.

"They've been needing an excuse to break the ice and be together for months. All I did was provide a time and place for them to meet and get past the awkwardness. From here on out, they're on their own."

"What will you do when they find out there wasn't really a study group session today?"

Elise shrugged. "I doubt they'll even bother looking into it. They'll probably be too occupied with each other to think it anything other than good fortune. If they come ask me, I'll just show them the schedule that says this room was reserved for their group. Their leader isn't very organized anyway. This isn't the first time one of their study sessions hasn't happened as scheduled. It's just the first time Clay and Shelby have been able to reap the benefits."

"Congratulations, Miss Hutchins. That's quite impressive. You've managed to successfully deceive two people and justify it as being for their own good. I don't know that I've seen a hardened criminal do such a brilliant job of appeasing his own conscience."

Elise met his eyes, and for a brief moment, she forgot to mask the hurt that was surely reflected in her own. Then she turned around and left.

This wasn't going to work. Ryan had already made his mind up about her, and now it was apparent that nothing she could say or do would change that.

Elise sped back down the staircase and to the front doors, attracting strange looks from those she passed. She didn't know if the attention was because she was obviously upset or because her wet hair was plastered to her scalp. She figured she must look terrible, but right now, she just wanted to make it to her car before she let loose in a good tear fest.

Ryan's hand on her upper arm stopped her right before she left the shelter of the library and headed back down the front steps and into the rain.

"Wait, Elise."

Elise turned around, but she kept her eyes lowered and focused on breathing deeply. If he said one more hurtful thing, she'd lose what little control she had left.

"I'm sorry. I shouldn't have said that. I agreed to give you twenty-four hours before I made any final judgments, and I still intend to do that."

Ryan's words and sincere tone brought Elise's head up to cautiously scan his face. His brow was furrowed in regret, and his hazel eyes were gentle, expressing concern for her.

"I know I can tend to be judgmental," Ryan continued with a grimace. "I guess it's a side effect of the job. But the real problem is probably that I feel very disillusioned about you. My impression of you was that of a nice, shy, Christian girl with great integrity. Then to find evidence to the contrary has shaken me. I'm not accustomed to being wrong in reading people."

In almost a reflex, Elise opened her mouth to defend her character, but Ryan held up his hand to stop her.

"That being said, you were right. All of my opinions of you so far have not been based on first-hand experience. I haven't given you a chance to defend yourself. So if the offer still stands, I would like to give you that opportunity. And I will do my best to keep from handing down a verdict until this time tomorrow."

Elise was quiet a moment. She was never one to hold a grudge. And, although she was still afraid that, in the end, his opinion of her wouldn't change, she had to at least try.

"Do you have plans tonight?" Elise asked.

"No," Ryan replied hesitantly, appearing a bit wary of her sudden subject change. "But I thought you were just talking about tomorrow afternoon."

"No, that would be a waste of a good eighteen hours," Elise replied with a smile. "I still have plans for tonight. I need to run home and change clothes, but can you meet me at the Paramount Theatre? I'll leave a ticket for you at the Will Call. The show starts at 7:30."

Though still reluctant, Ryan agreed.

As Elise left him and ran across Red Square once more, she realized that Chandra had gotten her wish. For as much as Elise longed to go to the show by herself, she had a date.

Chapter 6

The downside of being in her seat at the theater early was that Elise then had to nervously wait for Ryan. Would he even come, or would he just not show up? Then, if he did come, would he find her other matchmaking ploys unethical as well? Added to this was the knowledge that Ryan was an extremely attractive man, and she was going to have to sit close beside him for the entire duration of the show. And that was enough to make her shaky and a little nauseous.

Elise didn't date much. It might be more accurate to say she didn't date at all. She never had. Being brutally honest with herself, she knew her lack of a social life was really her own fault. Even after all these years, she was still painfully shy. If a man happened to glance her way, which didn't seem to occur very often, she ducked her head and pretended to ignore him. Yes, she knew it was childish. And yes, she sometimes got really mad at herself over it. But she could never seem to talk herself out of her same reclusive behavior. She could acknowledge full responsibility and blame, and yet she felt helpless to change.

Elise reached her hand to the back of her hair, checking to make sure no stray hairs had escaped the loose up-do. She shivered. It was cool in the theater, and even though she'd worn her white shawl, the material of her dress wasn't exactly designed for winter wear. But Elise had wanted to look nice. Her vanity and sense of fashion had won out over comfort when she'd put on her delicately embroidered white gown. As much as she wanted to deny it, she'd worn her best for Ryan.

Although Elise kept reminding herself that this was not a date, it still didn't help her apprehension. As silly as it sounded, Elise wanted Ryan to like her; not necessarily romantically, she was too realistic for that. But she did want to have his respect. Knowing that anyone would question her character and think so ill of her was extremely hurtful. Knowing that someone was just about the most handsome man she'd ever seen made it even worse.

"So what's the mission, Cupid?" the quiet voice at her ear startled her.

Their seats were close to the aisle, and Ryan had seized the opportunity of the empty seats behind her and snuck up.

Obviously enjoying her reaction of surprise, Ryan came around the aisle and slid into the seat beside her. "So we're seeing 'Warhorse'? I've heard it's a great show. But I somehow don't think you invited me here to trick me into a date. Though, considering your record, maybe you would?"

Elise knew he was teasing, but she couldn't help the wide-eyed blush she knew flooded her face. She would have never tricked Ryan into a date with her, but that didn't mean the mere sight of him didn't send her heart aflutter. Whether at church or the library, Elise had always seen Ryan in a suit. Tonight was no different, except that it looked to be a more formal suit, a tux. And the man made that tux look incredible.

Taking her reaction as a denial, Ryan continued. "So if the pleasure of my company isn't your purpose, why are we here?"

Elise handed him a pair of opera glasses. "Look below, at the orchestra level, about halfway between us and the stage."

Elise waited while Ryan tried to locate their target. She had chosen their seats well. They would have a great view of the stage and the matchmaking scene Elise had planned It was a beautiful, massive theater with gorgeous architecture that had a way of making one feel wealthy and elegant simply by being there. The soft glow of the lights made everything look golden, and Elise could easily develop a crick in her neck from studying the beautiful artistic detailing on the ceiling. Everything considered, it was a very romantic setting—perfect for what Elise had planned.

"Is that… the youth minister from church?"

"Yes, Clint Evers is our youth minister," Elise admitted as she lifted up her own pair of binoculars. "Oh, good. Here she comes up the aisle on the right."

"Who?"

"Janice Pasco. She also goes to church. I'm sure you've at least seen her in passing at some of the singles functions."

Ryan was silent as they both watched with rapt attention as Janice found her seat beside Clint. Clint immediately stood up, his body language showing his surprise and his smile showing his pleasure. After speaking for a few moments, both Clint and Janice sat in their seats, but their faces remained turned toward each other in a conversation that painted both of their expressions with what could only be described as a glow.

"So they obviously didn't come together," Ryan surmised, lowering the glasses. "I take it you arranged a 'chance' meeting."

Elise nodded. "Clint has liked Janice for a while now, but she had a boyfriend. The boyfriend was a jerk and didn't treat Janice well at all. They finally broke up a few months back, but it left Janice very hurt and fearful of relationships. Clint has wanted to ask her out for a long time, but now he's afraid it's too soon. He doesn't want to be the rebound guy, but he isn't sure how long Janice will need to heal. Janice likes Clint, but she's so nervous after her last relationship that she's not sure she can handle another one. She's already come a long way since her breakup, but now both she and Clint seem at a stalemate. Both are waiting for some kind of sign from the other, and both are terrified of giving that sign."

"So how did you get them both here?"

Elise took a deep breath. Ryan wasn't acting offended, at least so far. He just seemed interested. But she knew that if he was going to object, it would be over her methods.

"They both love theater, and they really wanted to see 'Warhorse,' which of course, has been sold out for a while. I sent each of them a ticket, saying in a note that it was a gift given by someone who wished to remain anonymous. Neither one of them knew the other one was coming. It's my hope that, after having the opportunity to 'accidentally' spend the evening together and enjoy the show, they'll be able to continue the relationship on their own."

"How do you know all this stuff, Elise? I mean this is personal. Their likes, their histories. Not to mention their attraction to one another. Do you have some kind of magic power over people that they will automatically open up to you, or are you actually a mind reader?"

Elise shrugged. "I'm not a mind reader, but I guess I'm pretty good at both watching and listening."

"But how do you even know they like each other?"

"Isn't it obvious? Even now, you can look at their body language like their goofy smiles and the way they are using exaggerated hand gestures. If you're close to them, you can also see the attraction in their eyes. I read once that if someone feels attraction, the pupils of their eyes dilate. I guess I'm good at picking up that kind of thing."

"But what about the details? How do you set something like this up? How did you know they both wanted to come to this show? How do you even know Janice is ready?"

"I talk to them some, and I observe a lot. Janice is ready, but just scared."

The lights dimmed, and the show began. Elise had always liked theatre, and although she'd come to see the fruits of her matchmaking efforts, she'd also wanted to see 'Warhorse' for herself. The artistry and choreography were amazing, and the use of puppets was spellbinding. She was soon so enthralled with the performance that it was almost as if she was in the world portrayed on the stage, forgetting about the reality of Ryan beside her and Clint and Janice below.

At numerous points, tears streamed down her face. She was aware that Ryan kept glancing at her. Feeling embarrassed, she tried to unobtrusively wipe the moisture away and stop their flow, but it was no use. Finally, Ryan reached over and captured her hand in his. Though she knew it was just a comforting gesture, Elise still lost track of the action on stage for several minutes while she tried to adjust to the warm pressure of her hand in his and the tingling sensations it sent up her arm.

By intermission, she already felt emotionally drained on every level.

"I didn't know this show was *this* sad!" Elise said, taking a deep cleansing breath as the lights came up. "I never saw the movie or read the book. Maybe it wasn't such a good idea for Clint and Janice's first date."

Ryan gently released her hand. "Don't worry. It ends well. I've both read the book and seen the movie. Besides, it looks like it was the perfect choice for Clint and Janice."

Elise looked down in the direction of Ryan's nod. Pulling up her binoculars, she took a closer look, not sure if she should believe her eyes. Clint had his arm around Janice in comfort as their heads tilted close together in conversation. Elise felt a surge of satisfaction. It looked as if Clint and Janice were going to be just fine.

Ryan stood and stretched. "Thank you for bringing me, by the way. Besides the matchmaking entertainment, it's a good show. I've wanted to see if for a while now. How did you happen to have an extra ticket for me anyway? Did you have to cancel plans with some hot date and give the ticket to me instead?"

Elise stood as well and began stretching her muscles to work out the kinks from sitting so long. Many of the other people around them had already moved toward the lobby and the restrooms, but Ryan made no move to follow.

Elise explained, "I bought four tickets initially—two for Janice and Clint, one each for me and my friend, Chandra. I like to see how my matchmaking scenarios turn out. I always figure if things go badly, I may need to be there to explain and smooth things out. Thankfully, I've never had to step in, but I do like to have that insurance. Mostly I like to know if the match is successful. I never orchestrate more than one Cupid scenario for a couple, and it's fun to—"

"Spy," Ryan filled in.

Elise shrugged. Why did he always have to make her actions sound so evil? "I guess if you want to call it that. I just enjoy seeing if all my work has paid off and witnessing that big moment in the lives of two people."

"So your friend Chandra obviously knows what you do. Did you have to cancel on her so I could have the ticket?"

"No, Chandra couldn't come because her little boy is sick. She called earlier today to cancel.

Yes, Chandra knows. She's gone with me a few times on Cupid errands."

"I still appreciate the ticket. You probably could have gotten a date to go with you if you hadn't felt the need to bring me along."

Elise didn't know what to make of this man. One minute he seemed to be criticizing her for "spying," and the next, he was sounding grateful and almost apologetic. "I'm glad you're enjoying it. There's no reason to thank me. The ticket would have just gone to waste if you hadn't used it. I didn't have any intention of asking anyone else. I don't date."

"You don't date?" Ryan repeated, obviously confused.

"No, not really. Why do you look surprised? Everyone always looks surprised when I say I don't date. Maybe I would if I ever got asked out, but I don't."

"So you're a matchmaker, yet you can't make your own match"

Elise shrugged. I guess I try to give to others something I figure I'll never have for myself."

"I guess you are a bit unapproachable," Ryan mused, studying her thoughtfully. His speculative gaze made Elise more than a little uncomfortable, and she fought the urge to squirm. "You send off first impressions of being very smart. You're shy, quiet, and not unattractive. Other guys are probably very intimidated."

"Not unattractive" might not seem a flattering term, but since Elise was typically a wall flower at social events, she didn't have much opportunity to receive compliments. Just the thought that Ryan found her "not unattractive" was enough to turn her cheeks a rosy shade of pink.

Some of the other people had begun filtering back into their seats. Not knowing how to respond, Elise sat back in her chair and picked up her binoculars, feigning a renewed interest in Clint and Janice in an effort to mask the sudden, awkward silence.

Elise spent the next several minutes watching the happy couple as they continued talking. It didn't look as if they had broken eye contact the entire intermission. Ryan didn't attempt to start a new conversation, though Elise could feel a strange tension building up in him. Did it bother him that she was "spying" on Clint and Janice?

The lights flickered, signaling that the show would soon resume.

Elise suddenly felt the startling sensation of Ryan's arm sliding across the back of her shoulders. She felt the hairs on the back of her neck stand on end as a shiver raced through her from head to toe. What was he doing?

As she turned to try to read his face, the lights in the theater dimmed, blinding her until her eyes adjusted.

The play resumed, and though she tried to focus on the action, she couldn't ignore that arm that remained around her shoulders. It wasn't as if he was stretching; it was almost a gesture of possessiveness, as if she really was his date. Tension still emanated from Ryan, and when he readjusted his arm so that his hand could drape across and gently rub her opposite shoulder, Elise couldn't take it anymore.

Chapter 7

"What are you doing?" Elise hissed, trying to be subtle for the sake of those around them. She was not one for confrontation, but she wasn't going to be able to pay attention the rest of the show at all if that arm continued in its unexplained mission.

Ryan bent his head close, his warm breath tickling her ear as he replied. "You see that guy across the aisle? He hasn't stopped ogling you since he returned to his seat at intermission. I didn't think he was the kind of guy you'd want paying attention to you, so I thought to make it clear to him that you were with me."

A flat denial was the first thing that jumped to Elise's lips. "Ogling me? No he isn't!"

But then she looked across the aisle. The man had to be at least in his forties with only a fringe of hair encircling his bald head. As she watched, he shifted slightly and glanced back at her. He had a beard and glasses. As their eyes met briefly, Elise felt a chill race through her. He didn't smile or even blink; he just looked at her. Maybe it was just because Elise wasn't accustomed to receiving male attention, but something about it made her nervous in a way she couldn't quite explain.

So Elise snuggled closer to Ryan and grabbed his free hand. She thought she heard a quiet chuckle as he willingly pulled her close. Before too long, Elise had forgotten about the unwanted attention and was once again engrossed in the show, though she could never fully tune out the awareness of Ryan's close proximity or the delightful sensations created by his warm touch.

Ryan was right; the show had a good ending that once again left Elise in tears. Afraid that Ryan would think her to be an overly-emotional female, she frantically wiped at her tears while Ryan flashed his dancing hazel eyes and the occasional grin. Much to Elise's frustration, he seemed to be thoroughly enjoying her reaction.

Curtain call and standing ovation over, Ryan once again captured Elise's hand to lead the way through the crowd. Elise cast one more glance down to see Clint helping Janice with her coat. Though they didn't see Elise's would-be admirer again, Ryan kept a tight hold of her hand as they threaded their way downstairs, through the people, and out the front door.

"I'd like to walk you to your car, if that's okay," Ryan said once they were outside in the cool night air.

"Thank you," Elise responded. "I'd appreciate that." She was parked in a lot only a few blocks away, but she'd never liked walking alone at night, especially downtown. She very much appreciated Ryan's offer. As soon as they'd exited the building, Ryan had released her hand. Now, as they began walking down the sidewalk, she tried to shake off the lonely feeling by stuffing her suddenly cold fingers into her pockets.

"I think the bearded, bald guy got the message," Ryan assured, "but I still don't like the idea of you walking alone."

"He definitely creeped me out," Elise admitted. "I don't know why he was staring at me."

"I think he was pretty harmless. He probably just thought you were pretty and lacked the social graces to realize he was being rude. I just can't believe you didn't notice him before I mentioned it. I thought you were supposed to be extremely observant."

"I am!" Elise defended.

"Maybe you're just good at observing others, but you're blind when it comes to yourself. You said you never get asked out on dates, but do you even notice all the men who check you out? You're not as inconspicuous as you may think."

"What do you mean? Guys don't look at me like that."

"Yes, they do. I've seen lots of guys looking at you at church like they'd certainly like a chance to audition to be your match."

Did this mean that *he'd* been observing *her*? Why?

Ryan continued, "Maybe you should put less effort into the love life of others and more into your own. You might not even need to use deception for that."

Elise stopped. She'd had enough of the hot and cold messages she kept getting from Ryan. He'd just been holding her hand; now he was calling her deceptive.

"So that's what you still believe? After spending the evening with me, you still think the worst of my character?"

"I don't know what to think! You're nice. You're beautiful. You care about others and want to help people. You're obviously very successful at matchmaking. But I still can't get around the fact that your primary tool is deception. You may not come outright and lie to someone's face, but you still work to create a scenario where two people believe some lie that you've created. You manipulate people and mess with their lives without their knowledge or permission. I just can't see how all of that can be viewed as ethical."

Elise's mind had tripped when he'd first started speaking. Had he really just called her beautiful? She'd frantically tried to keep up with what he was saying, and by the end, the initial compliments had been drowned with negativity.

"That's kind of like the pot calling the kettle black," Elise shot back with a gleam in her eye. "Weren't you trying to make Mr. Bearded Bald guy believe a lie? You used *deception* to make him believe that we were a couple. Isn't that the same thing? By your reasoning, couldn't it be said that you *lied* to him?"

Ryan looked at her, obviously startled by her reasonable argument. "No," he replied slowly as if trying to think through the dilemma on the spot. "It's not the same thing. I pretended that we were together in order to protect you. Would you have rather I hadn't done that?"

"No, I was glad you were trying to protect me! But that's the exact same thing I do! I make matches to help others. Do you really think Clint and Janice, or any of the other couples I've successfully set up, would rather that I hadn't done it?"

They had reached Elise's car and stopped to face each other.

"Look, Elise, you know we don't agree on this. I don't see protecting someone in the same light as matchmaking! I told you that I would give you twenty-four hours, and I intend to stand by that. You asked me to reserve judgment until then, but now you already act like you're giving your closing remarks!"

Elise sighed. "You're right. You just so aggravate me!"

"I'm sure I'll have plenty of time tomorrow to aggravate you further. How about we meet around 1:00 at Kerry Park? I live right across the street from there, and I should be done with my meeting by then."

"That will work. Thanks for the escort tonight."

"You're welcome. Good night, Elise."

As Ryan walked away, Elise slid into her car, a soft smile on her lips. She may not have fully convinced Ryan yet, but she had definitely made progress. After all, earlier tonight, she'd been "not unattractive." But just now, she'd been "beautiful."

Chapter 8

Elise watched as Ryan jogged through the rain to her car. Opening the passenger side door of her Honda Civic, he slid into the seat, bringing with him the smell of Seattle dampness mixed with his own masculine scent.

"So what do you have planned for us today, Cupid?" he asked, flashing her a grin as he buckled his seat belt.

"Lots of big plans," Elise replied noncommittally. "It's Valentine's Day, which is typically one of my busiest days for matchmaking. That's why I always take it off work."

"I guess I never really stopped to think that some days might be better than others where matchmaking is concerned."

"People tend to feel their loneliness most around the holidays and Valentine's Day. I typically try to put in a little extra effort so at least a few people aren't alone. Besides, the holidays are usually viewed as very romantic, which doesn't hurt at all."

"So who's your first victim?"

"Victim? I help people. I don't victimize them. Why are you so against the idea of matchmaking? Are you generally opposed to people falling in love? Do you hate the Easter Bunny too?" Elise said, deliberately trying to detour the subject. She wasn't ready for Ryan to know her full plan yet. After all, she knew it sounded really bad, and he would surely object on the basis of the big picture without taking the time to learn the details.

"No, I'm not opposed to love or the Easter Bunny. I only have a problem with your deceptive methods. Maybe it's a side effect of my job. Because I have to deal with lying and deception at its worst, I don't have tolerance for it in any form."

"You're a lawyer, right? Elise asked. "But you're also in school? What is it that has caused you to become so cynical?

"I don't think I'm cynical as much as realistic. I've seen humanity at its worst, and I guess it's hard to recover from that."

"You must be in criminal law."

"I did a stint as a prosecuting attorney," Ryan admitted. "But most of my success has come with international law. Some of the worst examples haven't come from felons, but from wealthy, powerful people who seem to have little care for anyone other than themselves."

"Why are you still a lawyer if you hate it so much?"

Ryan looked surprised. "I don't hate it at all. I love it. I'm working on my doctorate right now. I also am an adjunct professor at the university. Because of my success, I'm frequently called upon as a consultant in international cases. That's what my conference call this morning was about. You're right in that I dislike seeing the worst of human behavior, but I love being the one to help defend and bring justice to those who would otherwise not have any."

Ryan sounded so honorable. With his experience, it was no wonder that he viewed her pitiful attempt to "help" in such a bad light. Once again, Elise felt the hopelessness of trying to convince him of her motives.

"Um… Elise, where exactly are we going?"

Elise recognized the slight thread of suspicion in his voice as he obviously seemed to notice where their direction was taking them. She couldn't put it off any longer.

"We're going to the prison."

"The prison!" Ryan exploded. "You're making a match at the prison? Are you crazy?"

"No, I am not crazy! I'm not making a match at the prison. We're just going to talk to one of the inmates."

"Why? You said you were matchmaking. Are you setting a match up for after an inmate is released?"

"No." Elise tried to remain calm. There was no way she could give a good explanation for this one. Ryan was just going to have to see it. "We're just talking to an inmate about her daughter. It won't take very long. The daughter is the one I'm helping."

"How do you even find these people? The headlines of the newspaper? America's Most Wanted?"

Elise sighed. Ryan wasn't going to make this easy in any way. "Our church has a prison ministry. I'm sure you've heard it mentioned. I met this woman while volunteering for that ministry. And, for your information, I don't use the headlines to pick my 'victims.' I just observe people at church, at the library, wherever. And then, if I'm thinking about helping a couple with a match, I pray about it. I try to make sure it's something God would want me to do."

"Just like you prayed for Britney and me?"

"I did pray about you and Britney!" Elise muttered.

"So who was wrong on that one, you or God?"

Elise was quiet, not even wanting to respond. She pulled into the prison parking lot, found a space, and parked the car. Finally, she spoke quietly. "I pray about every match I even think about making. There have been many times that I haven't gone ahead simply because I didn't have a peace about it. Britney is a very nice person. And she likes you very much. If I make a match in error, it's my mistake. Not God's. I try to take every precaution, but I'm not perfect. I believe I already apologized for that misunderstanding, but if not, I'll do it again. I'm sorry."

Ryan sighed heavily. "I don't know why you seem to bring out the worst in me. I'm really not normally so..."

"Irascible... judgmental... unforgiving... "

Ryan's eyes shot to hers, words of defense on his lips, but seeing the teasing light in her eyes, his eyebrow quirked up and his expressions softened.

"Guess I deserve that."

Elise unbuckled her seatbelt, got out of the car, and opened the door to the back seat so she could pull out a garment bag. Wanting to have her umbrella up first, she tried to open it, but the old, cheaply-made contraption was jammed and wouldn't fully extend. As she struggled, Ryan came up beside her and extended his own classy black umbrella over her as well.

Elise tossed her under-achieving umbrella back into the car, grabbed the garment bag, and began walking to the front entrance with Ryan and his umbrella remaining in close attendance beside her.

"What's this lady in for?" Ryan asked

"I don't know. I didn't even ask," Elise replied. "It's not important. She mentioned that she'd made some mistakes. But now she's anxious to finish her sentence so she can get back to her family and turn her life around. I think the church's ministry has really helped her, and she's committed her life to Christ. She's very nice. You would never think her a criminal."

"Everyone is capable of being a criminal. I haven't even decided on your guilt or innocence yet."

As if she needed a reminder.

"So tell me what we're doing here," Ryan urged once again, ignoring her silence. "How are you helping this inmate and her daughter?"

Elise could tell that Ryan was the type who liked to know the plan. It probably gave him a sense of control over the situation. It was very likely driving him crazy not to know every single last detail. And Elise kind of liked the thought of throwing this self-assured man even a little off-balance.

Right before the entrance, Elise stopped and turned to face Ryan squarely.

"I think I've really told you all you need to know right now. Like I said, I don't know much about Tricia other than she's a woman who needs a little help with her daughter. I have a plan to help her, so beyond that, I guess you're just going to have to trust me."

From the tension emanating from Ryan, Elise knew he wasn't happy about the situation, but he kept his moody silence the entire time as they went through security and were led to a windowless room to wait for Tricia. He remained quiet even then, though after about thirty seconds of waiting, he popped out of his chair and began pacing the room. Elise ignored him and pretended to inspect her nails until finally, the door opened and a security guard led a woman dressed in the standard prison-issue jumpsuit inside.

Tricia's eyes jumped from Elise to Ryan, and she stopped dead in her tracks.

"I didn't ask for a lawyer," she said in confusion. "Elise, I already told you I was guilty."

"No, Tricia," Elise hurried to explain. "He's not here for—"

"How did she know I was a lawyer?" Ryan interrupted in confusion.

"Isn't it obvious?" Elise said, pointedly looking at Ryan from head to toe. "Wikipedia probably uses your picture to help define the term 'lawyer.'"

In Ryan's defense, Elise had to admit he wasn't dressed as a typical lawyer, at least not today. This was the first time Elise had seen him in anything other than a suit. But even with his khaki pants and forest green pullover, Ryan still had the unmistakable presence of a successful attorney.

"He is a lawyer, Tricia, but he's not here on official business. Ryan is my..." How exactly was she supposed to explain Ryan's presence? "friend," she finally finished. "He's just tagging along on my errands today."

Thankfully, Tricia seemed to accept this explanation and sat down at the table.

Elise stood and opened the garment bag. "Tell me what you think of this, Tricia. Do you think

Macy will like it?" Elise pulled out a beautiful turquoise blue gown. It had little cap sleeves and delicate sparkly detailing along the bodice. The classic empire waist extended in a long skirt made from soft flowing material.

Tears filled Tricia's eyes, and she suddenly couldn't speak around the emotion clogging her throat. Elise reached over and gently held the other woman's hand in quiet comfort.

"It's beautiful." Tricia finally managed. "It's perfect. Exactly what I imagined." Taking a few more cleansing breaths, she nodded more confidently. "She'll love it. But I'm sure you spent way too much money."

"Don't worry about that," Elise said firmly. "It was my pleasure."

Tricia got a little choked up. "I don't know how to thank you," she whispered brokenly.

"You don't have to." Elise replied. "I enjoyed doing it."

Worry suddenly creased Tricia's brow. "I know she'll love it, but I'm still worried that she'll refuse to go without a date. I know how much she wants to, but I also know my daughter can be extremely stubborn at times. She might find it too embarrassing to go to the dance alone."

"Don't worry," Elise assured. "I already have that covered. I've arranged for my cousin to escort her. They go to the same high school, so it will work out well. I helped him get a good grade in Trigonometry, so he owes me a favor."

"But is he a nice boy? Will she even like him? Macy is shy, and I hate to think of her feeling pressured to go out with a boy she doesn't like; or worse, one who doesn't behave well."

"He is very nice. He's a Christian and goes to the same church I do. I think they will like each other a lot. I wouldn't have asked him to go with her if I didn't think it would be good for both of them."

Tricia nodded. "Okay. Thank you, Elise. I will find a way to pay you back someday."

"The only payment I'll accept is you finishing your time here, getting back to your family, and living your life for God."

Tricia looked Elise in the eye. "With God's help, that's exactly what I intend to do."

Tricia walked back to the guard to be escorted back to her cell.

"I'll take pictures for you, Tricia, "Elise called. "I'll try to stop by next week to show you."

Tricia looked back, her eyes once again filling with tears.

"Thanks, Elise. I think you must be an angel."

As the door closed behind Tricia, Elise heard Ryan. "You know, she's not that far off, Cupid."

Ryan had been so quiet during the exchange, she had almost forgotten he was there. She packed the dress back in the garment bag, and moved to leave the room. She didn't dare look Ryan in the eye to try to read his response to her latest endeavor. She had to fulfill the next phase of this mission, and she couldn't waste time being distracted.

As they left the room, Elise finally replied. "No, I think for this task I deserve a different title."

Since they were preoccupied getting back through security, Ryan lost the chance to question her about what she meant.

Forty minutes later, they stood at the front door of a two story house that looked as if it had seen better days. An elderly woman answered in response to the doorbell.

"Hi, I'm—"

"Elise Hutchins," the woman finished, her eyes sparkling. "Patricia told me you would be coming. Thank you so much for what you're doing for my daughter and granddaughter. Please, come in. I haven't told Macy anything. The poor girl's been moping around all day."

As Elise and Ryan came in, the lady bustled partway up the stairs, not giving them a chance to get a word in. "Macy, come down here! You have guests!"

A pretty teenaged brunette appeared at the top of the stairs. Her brow wrinkled in confusion at the sight of the two unfamiliar people.

"Hi, Macy," Elise said with a gentle smile. "Your mom sent me. I'm your fairy godmother."

Chapter 9

"My mom actually sent this for me?" Macy asked, fingering the delicate material of the beautiful dress she wore as Elise helped her try on the gown in the teen's room upstairs.

"Yes," Elise replied, zipping up the back. "I met your mom through a program my church offers at the prison. She told me how much she wished she could be here to get you a dress for the Valentine's Day dance at your school. I think she mentioned that you'd just turned 16, and this was supposed to be your first real dance. I offered to bring a dress to you since she couldn't. So she described exactly what she wanted for you, and I went shopping. I took the dress to show her earlier today."

"I didn't think I would get to go," Macy said tearing up. "Grandma didn't have the money for a dress."

"Well, you are going," Elise said, gently pushing her so she could see herself in the full-length mirror hung on the back of her bedroom door. "And see how beautiful you'll look?"

Macy covered her mouth in shock as she stared at herself in the mirror. Tears now flowed in earnest down her face.

"It fits perfectly!" Elise said, pleased that the dress seemed tailor-made for the girl's trim figure. Macy was so distracted that she didn't even seem to notice the sound of the doorbell, which Elise was grateful for. Her job would be easier if Macy wasn't aflutter with nervousness.

"Get all your tears out now," Elise ordered gently. "We still have to do your hair and makeup, and we can't have you crying away all my fairy godmother magic."

Elise was by no means a beautician, but she'd had two younger sisters who had depended on her hair and makeup skills for all of their social functions in high school and beyond. Elise soon had her satchel of supplies spread across Macy's bed and went to work curling hair and applying a subtle sheen of cosmetics that only enhanced Macy's natural beauty.

"I'm almost done," Elise soon announced, twisting one last brunette curl into place at the top of Macy's head. "You should have plenty of time to get something to eat before the dance starts. And your mom left strict instructions that you had to be home tonight by 11:00."

Macy suddenly paled beneath her makeup. "I can't go!" she suddenly announced. "All my friends have dates. I told them I wasn't going. I can't show up alone! It would be humiliating to stand in the corner all night. Nobody's going to ask me to dance. Everyone already has someone to dance with!"

"You aren't going alone, Macy. I heard the doorbell ring before we started on your hair. He's probably downstairs waiting for you right now. You two are going to dinner and then the dance. Afterward, he'll bring you back home. He's very nice and responsible. I'm sure you'll like him."

"I have a date?" Macy asked, her brown eyes wide. "Who is he? You didn't get some old guy who thinks I'm a charity case, did you? Oh no. It's my brother, isn't it? You got Justin to take off work to help his poor, pitiful sister."

"No, to all those questions. He goes to your school. Maybe you already know Jake. Jake Kendry?"

"Jake Kendry? My date is Jake Kendry?" Macy let loose an excited squeal of pure childish delight. "Tell me you're not teasing me! Jake is a senior! And he's not just any senior! He's popular, plays on the football team, and is the class president! And he's hot!"

Elise had a hard time controlling her laughter. "I see you already know Jake," she managed to reply with only a slight grin.

"Know him? I practically love... well, I don't know that you can say 'love;' I am only sixteen. But I am pretty deeply infatuated with him."

Watching the play of emotions across Macy's face, especially the look of false maturity as she'd diagnosed herself as being "infatuated," was almost Elise's undoing. Macy's biography of Jake, along with the squeal of joy and her own words, made it incredibly difficult to maintain a straight face.

Elise cleared her throat. "Well, I think you're ready. Take a look at yourself in the mirror. And remember: no tears this time."

Macy's joy couldn't be contained. She pirouetted in front of the mirror and did a little dance like she was a three-year-old girl wearing her first princess dress. "Wait a minute," she said, coming to a complete stop. "Jake's downstairs *right now*? What if he doesn't think I'm pretty? What if he doesn't like me?"

"He will like you. And you are beautiful," Elise reassured. "Now, let's go. You don't want to keep him waiting.

Elise urged Macy back downstairs before the girl could torture herself more with nervous second thoughts. Thankfully, Macy was so excited, she hadn't even bothered to ask how Elise had managed to get Jake to take her to the dance. Elise knew it would make Macy feel more special if she didn't know Jake was doing it as a favor to his cousin.

Macy's entrance was all the fairy tale a teenage girl could dream. She floated down the staircase to meet her handsome (or hot, as she'd put it) date. He looked up. They made eye contact. He smiled and held his hand out to assist her the last few steps.

"I don't know that we've met officially, Macy, but I'm Jake."

"Hi, Jake," a bright-eyed, pink-cheeked Macy replied. "Thanks for taking me tonight."

"It's my pleasure. I should be thanking you for going with me. With the way you look in that dress, I'm going to have some serious competition by the end of the night."

Macy beamed.

Grandma was openly blubbering into an old-fashioned handkerchief. Camera at the ready, Elise snapped some pictures both of Macy alone and Macy and Jake together.

Elise felt movement at her elbow and turned to find Ryan's presence pulling her down to reality. She didn't want to think about how he was interpreting this scenario. She just wanted to enjoy that she had made a girl and her mother happy even if for just a little while.

But after a few moments of ignoring him, Elise realized she had to know what Ryan was thinking. He had waited downstairs the entire time she'd helped Macy. Now knowing the full extent of her plan and the results, did he still find it deceptive and unethical?

She darted a glance up to find him already looking at her. Was she just imagining it, or did his gaze hold a trace of admiration and… respect?

With a slight smile, Ryan slowly, deliberately bent down, moved Elise's dark hair ever so slightly away from her ear, and whispered, "Good job, Cupid."

Elise's heart immediately shot off in a hundred meter dash. She looked up at him, trying to find any trace of sarcasm. Before she could make a complete assessment, Macy and Jake were saying goodbye, eager to be on their way.

With one last hug for her grandma, Macy was soon out the door. Suddenly, she paused on the steps, turned, and ran back to Elise, enfolding her in a quick, fierce hug. "Please tell my mom 'thank you,'" she whispered.

This time, Elise was the one struggling to hold in the tears as she watched Cinderella ride away in Jake's little blue Toyota pickup truck.

Chapter 10

Ryan spoke quietly. "What happens when Macy figures out you bribed your cousin to take her to the dance? Won't she be hurt?"

They were sitting in a booth at a diner. After gathering her supplies and leaving Macy's house, Elise had driven here. Having not taken time for lunch, she was really hungry. But if Ryan was going to play twenty questions, she didn't know if she would be able to eat.

"I didn't bribe Jake," she explained. "Yes, he agreed to do it as a favor to me. But he'll like Macy. I did my homework on her. She's a nice girl who makes good grades. Though she and her siblings have had a rough few years, they're going to church now with their grandma, and I have a feeling their mother will soon come home changed for the better."

"Macy has siblings?"

"Yes. Her older brother was at work, and I think her younger sister was at a school basketball game. I wish I could have done more for the others. I know they've all got to be hurting with having such a difficult past and their mom being in prison. Somehow helping Macy doesn't seem enough."

"I don't think Macy and her mom feel that way at all. From what I saw, you did a very special thing for them today."

Elise looked into Ryan's eyes, trying to find the sarcasm or reproof she knew should be there. But she found none. She only saw honesty and could it be... admiration?

Did he actually admire her? Did he agree with her actions? Had she won him over?

Before she had time to search out the answers to her questions, they were interrupted by the arrival of their food. Elise had ordered tonight's special of grilled lemon rosemary chicken with rice and steamed vegetables. Ryan had ordered the chicken fried steak. One of the reasons Elise liked this diner was that they had rather a wide variety of unique, but delicious, meals on their menu. Elise felt they did a good job of serving upscale food at a casual price and atmosphere.

They ate in silence for a few moments, but soon Ryan took up where he left off in twenty questions.

"So do you do this kind of thing often? I mean, is this the first time you've done something like you did for Tricia and Macy?"

"Yes and no," Elise said, contemplating his question. "I haven't done anything exactly like this before, but I have done other small favors for inmates involved in our church's ministry. I've sent flowers for Mother's Day—that sort of thing. Usually in the spring, I have a lot of fun working with a charity that helps underprivileged teenage girls get dresses and makeovers for prom. It's like I get to be a fairy godmother for that one too. But I guess this is the first time I've ever combined the prison ministry with a Cupid scenario."

Elise looked at Ryan and grimaced. "That sounds really bad, doesn't it?"

Ryan grinned and shrugged. "You don't normally mix matchmaking with convicts, but I must admit, this time it seemed surprisingly successful. Now will you follow up with Macy and Jake? I know you said before that you leave people on their own after your initial help."

"I'll take the pictures to the prison to show Tricia. And I'll ask Jake about it, but I won't interfere any more in his relationship with Macy. If Tricia or Macy need help with something else, I'll do what I can. This isn't really a typical Cupid scenario. But I guess every match I make is unique in some way. If there wasn't something special about each case, I wouldn't bother trying to help."

Pausing, she once again forced herself to make eye contact with Ryan. She usually made a point to always look people in the eye. But with Ryan, she seemed to find herself fearful of what she might find there. "Thank you, Ryan. I just left you downstairs at Macy's house without an explanation. You had to wait quite a while until I had her ready to go."

"I didn't mind. I talked to Macy's grandma, and then when Jake arrived, I talked to him. I wasn't bored. Macy's grandma is a sweetheart, and Jake is a great kid. I enjoyed talking to him. He's apparently very versed on sports of any kind…"

Elise smiled and nodded in the right places, but her attention had just been diverted. Others might only see the bustle of the busy restaurant. The décor was in the style of a classic diner, complete with red vinyl booths and a black and white highly-glossed tile floor. Though not dressed in uniforms, the waiters and waitresses did wear white shirts and black bottoms along with traditional little white aprons.

Most people probably wouldn't have even noticed the petite elderly lady who had just entered the restaurant. Looking around, the woman walked across the floor to take a seat alone in a corner booth. But Elise saw the lady, saw her red dress graced with a gold brooch at the neck, heard her high heels click faintly on the tile as she walked, saw her perfectly coifed hair that was probably loaded with half a can of hairspray, and saw her eyes scan the room and light up as they came in contact with the barstools at the counter.

As the lady slid into the booth, Elise glanced over in the direction of one particular barstool. And then she knew for sure.

Like background music, she could still hear Ryan droning on, but the words weren't processing. "... said he was looking to major in science and possibly discover how to create a food source out of rocks little green aliens left when they came to visit the Smurfs."

Ryan paused. "Elise... Elise, did you even hear a word of what I just said."

Elise's eyes flashed back to Ryan. "Oh, yes... Macy's grandma. Jake. Sports. Smurfs... Smurfs?

Wait a minute, maybe I wasn't listening as closely as I should! I'm sorry. What were you saying?"

Now Elise's attention focused fully on Ryan. She was mortified, and she knew her pink cheeks did nothing to hide her guilt.

"How about you just tell me why we're really here, Elise? I saw your eyes doing reconnaissance. Who were you looking at? Another victim? You have another match planned, don't you?"

"No. I mean, yes. I mean…" She winced. There was no way Ryan was going to like this.

"Are you always so deceptive? Why didn't you just tell me?"

"I didn't know! At least, not for sure."

She shut her eyes briefly, breathing a quick prayer. This was going to cost her. If she went through with this, she would surely lose all the points she may have earned with Ryan.

Then, as if in answer to her prayer, a sudden assurance filled her. She knew what she had to do.

"I come to this diner a lot," she explained calmly. "I've been watching some of the other regulars for a long time. There's an elderly lady behind you in the corner. Her name is Stella."

Ryan discreetly stole a glance behind him.

"Sitting at the counter on one of the barstools is an elderly man in a plaid shirt. His name is George."

She watched Ryan glance over at the counter and nod.

"George and Stella are both widowed and lonely. They've been smiling at each other and exchanging pleasantries for months. But, since they've both been out of the dating game for about fifty years, I don't think either one knows how to make the first move. If you look carefully, Stella has put herself in the perfect position to discreetly watch George, and George has angled himself to watch Stella. They do this every time. And it's really cute and funny to see how they catch each other stealing glances, and then they look away as if it never happened."

"So you've been planning to set them up." Ryan filled in.

"I've thought about it. I've prayed about it. I thought they might be here tonight, but I wasn't sure. That's why I didn't mention it sooner. I haven't felt like it was the right time. But when I saw each of them walk in tonight, I knew they both were ready."

"How did you know?"

"They're both dressed up in their best for Valentine's Day. Stella is wearing a red dress complete with high heels. George is wearing a nice shirt he obviously took time to iron. You should have seen the look of longing they sent each other without the other one noticing. I can tell that they're each hoping that the other will do something to show an interest."

"You're sure? What if you're wrong and they're dressed up for a special church service or even a funeral? What if they secretly hate each other or aren't ready to have a relationship with anyone?"

"I'm not wrong. I haven't really been a passive observer for this one. I've talked to both Stella and George on numerous occasions. They're good friends to me. I think they kind of look at me as a granddaughter. They would have already come over to say 'hi' except you're here with me. By their smiles and curious looks our direction, I can tell they think we're on a date and don't want to interrupt."

"So let's suppose you're right about their mutual attraction? What are you going to do about it? What's your plan to match Stella and George?"

Elise felt worry sneaking back into her mind, creasing her brow. This one act could ensure her guilty verdict from Ryan and result in the maximum sentence. Yet she had to be true both to herself and to Ryan. She couldn't let George and Stella experience another lonely Valentine's Day, especially not when she had the power to help change it.

Chapter 11

Elise didn't answer Ryan. Instead, she caught the eye of Amber, one of the waitresses passing by, and signaled her over.

"Hi, Elise, did you need something?" Amber asked.

"Amber, could you do me a favor? I'd like to pay for Stella's dinner tonight, but I don't want her knowing it was me."

"That's sweet of…" Amber started to say, but then stopped as understanding suddenly dawned on her face. Her eyes began to sparkle. "Oh, I get it! Do you want me to pretend it's from somebody else?" With a subtle wink, Amber made it clear that she knew exactly what Elise was up to. After all, it wasn't a secret that Stella and George were fond of each other. They had been providing reality entertainment for the diner staff for months.

"No, I don't want you to lie. Don't tell her who it is at all. Just let her believe what she wants."

"Should I wait to tell her when she gets her check?"

"No, just mention it when her food arrives. I think Susie is taking her order right now. But, knowing Stella, it'll probably just be her usual order of meatloaf."

"Got it. We should have done this months ago!" With that excited whisper, Amber hurried off to the kitchen.

Elise didn't need to be told that Ryan disapproved. The scowl on his face said it all.

"Won't it be obvious to Stella when Amber tells her someone paid for her meal?" he asked impatiently. "She was just here talking to you, and she hasn't talked to George at all."

"Amber is smart. She'll cover her tracks. She's probably getting the entire staff on board right now. Watching those two dance around each other for months has been driving them all crazy. My only concern is that they may be a little too eager with their assignment. Let's just wait and see what happens. You can criticize me later."

Ryan's only response was something that sounded halfway between a snort and a grunt.

Elise ignored him.

Fortunately, they didn't have long to wait. The waitress named Susie came out from the back and refilled George's water glass. Though they couldn't hear the words, the smiling waitress conversed with him a few moments before returning to the kitchen area. Ryan kept glancing at his watch. His impatience was setting her nerves more on edge than they already were.

Please, Lord. Let this work out!

Though Elise knew her pride was at stake, she also knew there was more riding on this outcome. The success of this match in no way guaranteed Ryan's approval. But if it failed, it did pretty much guarantee that Ryan would think the worst of her and probably go through with sharing her secret and ruining her reputation. But even harder to take than that result would be the knowledge that she had been wrong and she never should have interfered in the love lives of others. She had prayed about George and Stella, and if she was wrong this time in her interpretation of God's direction, then her entire paradigm unraveled. She could no longer say she'd been right about any of the others either. In short, her past, present, and future all depended on Stella and George.

Susie came back through the swinging kitchen doors carrying a plate and a basket of rolls. Amber came through the doors behind Susie, but made no move to follow the other waitress as she headed toward Stella's table.

Good girl, Amber! Elise thought, realizing Amber had undoubtedly enlisted Susie's help to throw off any suspicion.

Ryan suddenly stood from his position across the table from Elise. Elise looked up in confusion as he stepped forward and slid onto the bench right beside her. His sudden nearness made her heart trip over itself and she couldn't get her tongue untangled to ask what on earth he was doing.

"If you're going to make me sit through this, I at least need to be in a position to watch the silent movie," Ryan whispered defensively. "I don't have eyes in the back of my head to watch Stella from across the table."

Elise's relief was short-lived, for Ryan immediately slid his arm behind her shoulders and pulled her body even closer to his.

Elise looked at him in alarm.

"What?" he asked innocently, though his eyes clearly danced mischievously. Leaning over, he whispered in her ear. "I thought you wanted to avoid suspicion. I have to appear to have a reason for coming to this side of the table. What better reason than to look as if I have romantic intentions toward you. After all, you *are* Cupid and it is Valentine's Day."

Elise somehow got the distinct impression that Ryan was deliberately taunting her and enjoying every second of it. Was this some kind of sweet revenge for him?

Susie had already placed Stella's meal on the table and was talking to her. So instead of some brilliantly-fashioned retort to Ryan's behavior, Elise opted for the simple finger to the mouth with an accompanying, "Shhh."

Though they couldn't hear Susie's words, they saw the instant Stella understood the news. The pleased, shy smile couldn't be hidden and the delicate blush creeping into her cheeks couldn't be denied. As if watching a well-acted pantomime, not a word was audible, yet the events perfectly apparent. Elise watched as Susie shook her head in a negative motion, but then seemed to take what appeared to be an involuntary glance over her shoulder at George. Stella's blush grew even rosier. As Susie smiled and turned to leave, Elise was sure she saw the waitress shoot a wink back at Stella.

Walking back to the kitchen, Susie took the time to smile and say a few words to George while also directing a few pointed looks back Stella's direction.

"Well, that was an Oscar-worthy performance," Ryan said dryly.

"Susie should be an actress," Elise agreed, trying to hold in her laughter. That had been beautifully played. Although she was sure Susie had in no way lied about who was paying for Stella's meal, she had also obviously given the impression that it was George.

"And I'm sure you're ready to put your disclaimer all over that," Ryan said. "You weren't the one who deceived that poor woman. You can't help what other people choose to do."

"No, I'll take full responsibility for Susie's 'deception,'" Elise replied. "Though I didn't give specific instructions, she did exactly what I wanted her to. I just didn't realize she would be *that* good in the message delivery."

Ryan started to say something, but Elise cut him off. "Before you start criticizing me, you should stop your own deception and go back on your side of the table. I never asked you to pretend to be interested in me romantically. Couldn't you say that you were deceiving everyone in the diner?"

Ryan didn't move a centimeter away from her. He stayed in the exact same position with his arm around her shoulders, holding her close. Instead, he leaned over, his warm breath once again tickling her ear. "Who said I was pretending?"

Chapter 12

Elise met Ryan's hazel eyes and suddenly had difficulty swallowing. Every nerve in her body felt like it had been lit with an electric charge. She couldn't read the emotions she found in Ryan's gaze. Was he teasing?

She didn't understand him. One minute he was throwing stones at her character the next he was actually… flirting with her?

Elise tried to find her voice. But it was as if she suddenly couldn't remember how to speak. Ryan was returning her gaze with an assessing look himself, as if he was trying to gauge her response to his words.

Before Elise could wade through her emotions to make sense of anything, she caught movement out of the corner of her eye. Stella walked by their table. With a surge of excitement, Elise watched as the elderly lady headed directly toward George. Seeing the direction of her attention, Ryan turned to watch Stella's progress as well.

Looking around the diner, Elise had to work to control her laughter as she realized she and Ryan weren't the only spectators. As Stella neared George, it seemed as if all sounds and movement in the diner paused. Waitresses stopped in their duties, customers silenced their conversations, and Elise was sure she could see Amber and the cook peeping through the slats in the door to the kitchen.

George turned to Stella, sliding off the barstool and standing to his feet as she shyly approached him. Everyone in the diner seemed to be collectively holding their breath.

Straining her ears in the sudden quiet, Elise could hear Stella speak. "It seems rather silly that we're both dining alone. Won't you bring your plate over and join me, George?"

"Stella, I'd be delighted. The only thing more enjoyable than good food is good company."

With matching smiles that bordered on giddiness, they returned together to Stella's table. While they normally should have noticed being the center of attention, they were so absorbed in each other that they seemed oblivious to everything around them.

"Congratulations, Cupid," Ryan whispered beside her. "It looks like you just made another successful match."

"I hope so," Elise replied. "George and Stella deserve to be happy. But only time will tell."

"Won't they find out about the set up? Won't Stella try to thank George and the whole thing unravel?"

"No, Stella won't mention it. She knows George wished to remain anonymous. She's a classy lady. She won't draw attention to what she perceives as him being a gentleman. If she does happen to mention it at some point, they won't be upset by it. They'd probably even get a kick out of the kids at the diner trying to set them up. Believe me, they've both been waiting for this day. They'll seize this opportunity and be grateful for however means it was delivered."

Ryan still didn't look fully convinced, but Elise had a hard time regretting anything about what had just happened. George and Stella were happy, and that was what mattered to her.

Amber soon appeared with separate checks for their meals, as requested, and two decadent-looking hot fudge brownie sundaes.

"These are on the house and come with a big 'Thank you,' from the entire staff," she announced with a big smile.

"I should be the one thanking you and Susie," Elise replied.

"We were only too happy to help out. Now that you've made Valentine's Day special for George and Stella, along with the entire diner, I hope you two can make yours special as well." With a wink, Amber was gone.

"Why do I get the feeling you may just have created a bunch of monsters?" Ryan asked dryly. "Amber and Susie might have liked their task a little too much. I'm not sure Seattle can handle more than one Cupid. What am I saying? I've watched you all day, and I'm still not sure Seattle can handle even one Cupid. You were serious when you said Valentine's Day was a busy Day for you. You've given me a lot to think about."

"Oh, we're not done yet."

"What do you mean?" he asked suspiciously.

"We have one more stop before I let you go for the night. Hurry and eat your dessert; we're on a timeline."

To Elise's relief, Ryan didn't object, and fifteen minutes later, their hot fudge brownie sundaes had been devoured, and with Elise's brief wave at the happy couple, they were on their way.

The drive passed quickly, and Elise soon pulled into a parking space at a destination she knew would be undoubtedly recognizable to Ryan even in the dark of this time of night.

"Oh, no," Ryan groaned. "You set somebody up at the Space Needle, didn't you? I really didn't think you would be so cliché."

"There's nothing wrong with being cliché," Elise said defensively. "I think it would be very romantic to be surprised by a date at the Space Needle. But no, that's not why we're here. Do you know how expensive it is just to go up in that thing? This Cupid does have her limits. I try to avoid fancy restaurants, expensive tourist attractions, and the pressure that would go along with both. "Warhorse" was a definite splurge. Maybe someday I'll be able to set up that kind of date, but not now, especially with needing resources for other matches as well."

"Then why are we here?"

"You'll see," Elise said, once again wanting to keep her plans to herself as long as possible. The longer she waited to tell Ryan, the less time he'd have to object. "We need to hurry."

Ryan followed her as she walked directly beneath the Space Needle and then kept going. Elise finally entered a small shopping mall-type building and took a stairway to the second floor. The building was arranged so that the stores and restaurants were positioned around a center open area with hardwood flooring. A railing on the second floor bordered the open area so that people standing there could look down on it, almost like in a courtyard or stadium.

Immediately after reaching the second floor, Elise walked to the railing and looked down, scanning the area.

"There he is," she said under her breath.

She then took out her cell phone and dialed a number without a word of explanation to Ryan.

"Hi, Greg, this is Elise. I'm not going to make it tonight. I'm really sorry I didn't let you know sooner, but I've had a change of plans."

"Well, that stinks," Greg said. "I guess I'll just go home, and we can do it a different time."

"Oh, are you already there?"

"Yeah, I guess I got here a little early."

"No, please stay," Elise urged. "In fact, would you do me a favor? My friend Chelsie needs a partner. We usually have to dance together for the class because there aren't enough men to go around. I was going to share you tonight, but would you mind being Chelsie's partner? She's really nice, and

I'd feel really bad if she didn't have anyone for the class."

"I guess I could do that. I'm already here. What does your friend look like?"

"Chelsie is taller than I am with long, medium-brown hair and brown eyes. She usually wears a silver bracelet around her right wrist.

"Okay, I think I see her. I'd better go. The class is getting started, so I need to go introduce myself."

"Thank you so much, Greg! I'll owe you one."

"Don't worry about it, Elise. I've noticed you're always doing stuff for others. This is the least I can do. I'll talk to you later. Maybe I can come again next week and do the class with you."

Elise signed off and pressed "end." She felt Ryan's eyes on her.

"So that's how it's done?" he asked.

"We'll see," Elise responded. "Greg is the tall, blond guy with glasses down there. Chelsie is the pretty brunette sitting on the bench."

They watched as Greg walked up to Chelsie and introduced himself, holding out his hand to shake hers. After a few brief moments of conversation, Chelsie rose from the bench, and they both walked to the center of the court area where the class was getting started. There were about ten others in the class. Soon the music was echoing a through the space and the couples were swirling over the hardwood floor, learning the steps to the waltz.

"I should have brought my opera glasses," Elise muttered. The lighting in the building wasn't great, and from their angle looking down from a distance, it was difficult to see the expressions on the faces of the dancers. It looked as if Greg and Chelsie were having a good time. Every once in a while she would catch a glimpse of their smiling faces.

"Oh, it's hard to do any decent spying from afar?" Ryan asked.

Elise tried to ignore Ryan's comment but realized it was probably time for her to give him an explanation. Maybe Ryan wouldn't judge her so harshly if he knew the background to her actions. Because this was the first time Greg and Chelsie met, there probably wasn't going to be much to see anyway. Somehow, though, a familiar, awful feeling still nagged her. No matter what she said, it wasn't going to change Ryan's impression of her. He would still find her guilty.

Chapter 13

Though refusing to answer his sarcastic question about spying, Elise turned to Ryan and explained, "Greg is my dentist. Or, rather, he's my dentist's son. He took over the practice for his dad a few months ago. Since he just moved here recently, he's been looking to find things to do in the Seattle area. He's come to our church singles group a few times, but he was also interested when I mentioned this dance class I've been attending. It's just a casual thing. Whoever shows up on Thursday nights can participate. We've learned different types of ballroom dances and even swing and country line dancing. I met Chelsie here at class. She's like me, though. She comes alone and just takes the class for fun."

"So you decided to deceive Greg and set them up."

Elise winced. "I don't usually do blind set ups like this. The couples I match usually know each other, and I've had a chance to observe them interacting. I was originally just going to have Greg come with me and introduce him to Chelsie. But then I thought it might be better if I wasn't there, so it would be more natural than a formal introduction. It's always better if a couple doesn't know they're being set up. That way, there's a lot less pressure, and they feel more free to talk and get to know each other. It also helps that my absence kind of forces them together."

"So what's Chelsie's story? Why did you feel that she needed your help?"

"Chelsie's husband was in the military. About three years ago, he was killed in the line of duty. She and her son moved back here to Seattle to be close to her family. Her son, Liam, is five now. She is a physical therapist, and when she's not working, she's spending time with Liam. Her parents finally told her that she needed to get out and find some friends and a hobby. They watch Liam so that, one night a week, she gets a break and can come take this class. She's been through so much working through the grieving process. I would love to see her happy with someone else to love."

"I can see why you wanted to make a match for her. But I'm a little nervous about you matching her with Greg. Did you ever think that Greg may be interested in you? After all, you're the one he agreed to come dancing with?"

"No. We're just friends. I've mentioned to him the possibility of setting him up with one of my friends, and he was game."

"I can't imagine a single guy being interested in *just* being your friend," Ryan said quietly.

Choosing to ignore the undercurrent of Ryan's comment, Elise shrugged and replied, "I have a lot of guy friends, or maybe I should say guy acquaintances. I've been told I'm hard to get to know. I guess I still have the residual effects of being painfully shy. There's no attraction between Greg and me, so he's definitely in the friend category. He and Chelsie, on the other hand, are perfect for each other. They have a lot of similar interests, but she tends to be reserved, whereas he's more outgoing and adventurous. Since they've never met, though, I can in no way guarantee that it will work out. I guess it's just a hunch. I didn't see the harm in helping them each have a date for Valentine's Day, even if it is just one evening. I really think that they'll at least develop a good friendship out of this. Even if that's all that results, I'll consider it a success."

"And to you, that success is worth the tactics it takes to achieve it. The end justifies the means. You just lied to a man in order to set the poor, unsuspecting guy up on a blind date with a woman he's never met."

"I did not lie to him. I said I had a change of plans. And I already told you that I don't usually do it this way. I usually like to observe people who already know each other and then make arrangements for them to find each other. This isn't a typical match."

"You've said that before. For just about every match I've seen you do. They never are typical, are they?"

Elise looked at him. He wasn't angry; his tone was weary and maybe a little sad. And he was right. Every match she did was unique. She really couldn't say she abided by any rules because there were always exceptions. The only constant was her sense of integrity and her desire to act in a way that would please her Savior. And from Ryan's perspective, she had failed miserably at that.

Having no response, she turned back to the rail, and they were both quiet as they watched the dancing below a few more minutes. Elise saw Chelsie apparently step on Greg's toes. Even from this distance, their tinkling laughter flitted up to her ears like delicate butterflies being released from below.

"I'm ready to go if you are," Elise said, suddenly feeling very weary. Obviously, Greg and Chelsie had passed the awkward stage and were thoroughly enjoying their time together. "I don't think I'm needed here. They seem to be doing just fine."

Ryan nodded, and they walked back down the stairs and out into the Seattle night. They took a leisurely pace back past the Space Needle and to Elise's car. She kept waiting for Ryan to say something, to ask a question or make another sarcastic comment about this latest match, but he remained silent.

As she drove to take Ryan home, Elise kept waiting for him to speak. This was her last stop for the night. He'd known it was the last one. Why wasn't he asking questions or rendering a verdict? Her nervousness increased as Ryan's silence lengthened. Was he not going to say anything?

Elise pulled to the curb in front of Kerry Park. This is where she had picked Ryan up, but she wasn't sure which building was his.

Elise cleared her throat, trying to work up the courage to break the uncomfortable silence. "So I guess that's about it. I know I only said twenty-four hours, and it's been longer than that. I'm sorry. Thanks for sticking with me to the end. I appreciate you giving me this chance."

He must still think her a terrible person. Why else would he be so silent? He was probably trying to find a way to tell her that he was going to follow through with exposing her secret. Elise felt tears burning in the back of her eyes. She had hoped that, once he'd gotten to know her a little better, he'd understand her and not be so judgmental of her character. That had obviously not happened, and now she just wished he'd leave so she could cry.

In her mind, she kept hearing Ryan's tone as he'd said her matches never were typical. She didn't play by the rules, and to him, coloring outside the lines was not acceptable.

When she felt she couldn't stand the tension for one more second, Ryan finally spoke. "It's not raining like it was earlier today. This park has the best view in Seattle. Do you have time to get out and talk a minute?"

Chapter 14

It was a beautiful night. With the rain that had lasted most of the day and the late hour, the popular little park was nearly deserted. As they walked to the railing that bordered the overlook, Elise pulled her coat tight, thankful that the air was chilly but not miserably cold. The view of the city below was breathtaking. The Space Needle and the rest of the Seattle skyline stood outlined in lights against the black canvas of night.

"I doubt the view from inside the Space Needle could be more spectacular than this one from outside," Elise mused.

Ryan looked at her funny, but didn't comment. Elise had lived in Seattle for years, and yet she was probably the only resident in the city who had never been to the top of the iconic Space

Needle. She'd like to go someday, but she'd rather not go alone. So for now, this view from the park at the top of the hill was more than adequate.

Once again, Elise found herself waiting for Ryan to speak. He'd said he wanted to talk, but now it was as if they were both facing forward in an elevator, pretending that the other person didn't exist. After several moments, the view began to lose its soothing effect on Elise.

What was Ryan thinking about? Was he secretly delighting in torturing her with the silent treatment? Or maybe he was trying to think of how to give his guilty verdict without having her fall apart. Finally, she couldn't take it anymore. She decided on a preemptive strike.

"Look, Ryan. I know you dislike me. You think I manipulate people and purposely deceive them to suit my own whims. You saw the flowers Britney received as a lie from me because they had your name as the sender. And apparently, you'll never forgive me for that single sin against you."

Without pausing for breath, she continued in a rush, "Even after spending all this time with me, it's clear that you still think my methods unethical and doubt my character. But the truth is, I think you're judging me unfairly. I do not deliberately try to lie to people or deceive them in any way. My motive is to help. I do not make any matches lightly. I don't take any action without thought and prayer. Contrary to your opinion of me, I do not believe that the end justifies the means. I've actually struggled a lot with trying to balance my desire to help people by anonymously matchmaking with methods that do not compromise my integrity. I put a lot of effort into it. I would never want to hurt any of the people involved, and if I thought anyone would object, I would never make a match.

Elise paused, waiting for Ryan to respond. After about ten seconds without a response, she gave up and released all the other words that had been brewing inside. "I don't know how you can call it deception when those supposedly deceived would not want it any other way. Is it a lie if the people being lied to would not expect or want the truth? My grandmother died last year of Alzheimer's. Before she died, there were times my grandma would ask where my grandfather was. We had to knowingly lie to her, saying that he'd gone fishing for the day, when in reality, my grandfather passed away ten years ago. But it was kinder to lie to Grandma than tell her the truth and have her live once again a fresh grief she was not able to process.

"Likewise, if given the choice, I don't believe the couples I make matches for would want the truth, if that's what you want to call it. I do not deliberately lie to people. I present them with a scenario, and I let them choose to believe what they want. Even if a match doesn't work out, I've offered them the hope of a fairy tale, if even for a second. There is so much ugliness and hardship in the world, people want a little bit of fantasy and magic. They long for romance. They search for that special someone with the hope that something or someone will manipulate fate to help them find each other. They want the hope of an epic love story that will end in happily ever after. They need a Cupid."

As Elise's final words melted into silence, her heart was pounding with conviction, and yet, she had a strange peace as well. It was the peace of knowing she had laid her heart bare and said what needed to be said.

"That was a very good closing argument, Elise," Ryan said seriously.

"What?" Elise responded, thoroughly confused.

"Yesterday you asked me to allow you a defense. Just now, you gave a beautifully worded, wonderfully executed argument for your case."

"It doesn't matter how the case was presented or how good the closing argument was," Elise responded. "What matters is the verdict."

Ryan nodded his head but didn't speak.

Come on! Elise thought, anticipating another lengthy silence. *Tell me what you're thinking!*

"How do you see me, Elise?" Ryan asked abruptly. At her look of confusion, he explained. "You're so good at observing others. You seem to have a gift for being able to see who people really are, their motivations, their character. You know what they're thinking and feeling. Where others only see what's on the surface, you look deeper to find out who someone is, and then you do whatever you can to meet his or her desires and needs. So, I'm curious. What have you observed about me? How do you see me?"

Elise's brain fumbled to catch up with the unexpected subject change. "You confuse me," she replied honestly, saying the first thing that popped into her head. "You're right in that I'm usually very good at reading people, but I have a really difficult time reading you. I can never tell what you're thinking. One minute you seem to despise me; the next you're looking like you respect and possibly even admire me."

"But how do you see me?" he repeated. "What kind of man am I? What do you observe in me?"

Elise wasn't exactly sure what he wanted from her. So, blowing out an exasperated breath, she let him have it all. "You're arrogant, judgmental, and harsh. You're stubborn and quick to jump to conclusions. Once you form an opinion, it's practically impossible for it to be changed or revised. In your world, there is no gray; everything is black or white, good or evil. But at other moments..." Elise's voice softened and grew more thoughtful. "I also see glimpses of a different man. You're kind, teasing, light-hearted. You're thoughtful, loyal, intelligent. You have high values and a strong love and faith in God. You're a man of integrity who's willing to fight for justice and unwilling to turn his head to ignore evil. You're a man to be admired."

Ryan stared out at the Seattle skyline, seeming to avoid eye contact with Elise. Had she gone too far? Maybe she shouldn't have mentioned all that bad stuff.

He responded, "It's funny to me that you can be so good at observing other people and their relationships and so bad about knowing how others view you. I am arrogant, judgmental, and all the rest of what you just mentioned. You're right about me in all areas except one." He turned and looked her directly in the eyes. "You apparently have no idea how I see you."

"What do you mean? How do you see me?"

"You think I confuse you, but like you, I'm also a very good judge of character. I have to be as a lawyer. But I've never been more confused about someone in my life. You are a mystery to me that I can't figure out. You're right that I see everything in black and white. When I look at your matchmaking on the surface, it seems that you manipulate events and people to achieve your own ends. The tactics you use are borderline at best. There's no difference if you knowingly lead someone to believe something you know to be false or if you verbally tell the lie yourself. You have no right to meddle in people's lives like that, especially in their love lives. They haven't asked you to, and it almost seems like you're messing around with God's job of bringing two people together on His terms.

Ryan's hard gaze soften with a gentele glow as he gave a careful study of Elise. "But on the other hand," he admitted, "you've forced me to follow you around and take a deeper look at who you are and what you do. I've seen a completely different picture. I see how God uses you to bless others and show His love and purpose in their lives. I've seen a woman with high morals and values who has gone out of her way to help everyone from a prison inmate to a lonely elderly couple, from high school and college students to a youth minister, a widow, and a dentist. You can be aggravating, stubborn, and manipulative. And yet, you are endearing, shy, and kindhearted. You're unlike any woman I've ever met, and I'm completely… fascinated."

"You make a pretty decent closing argument as well," Elise said with a smile. "But what does that mean? You can understand my motives, but still can't appreciate all my methods. You're complicated. I'm complicated. We probably won't ever agree on everything. So is that a 'Not Guilty' verdict?"

Ryan frowned. "After seeing everything over the past day, I can honestly say that I'm okay with everything you've done. I may not have done it myself, but I can view it as a gray area and understand that not everyone may agree with me. However, there's one action I still cannot excuse. The first one. You sent flowers to Britney and signed my name. There's no way that's a gray area. That was just an outright lie."

"I'm sorry, Ryan, I have no excuse for that one, and I won't even attempt to justify it. All I can do is apologize profusely and promise you that I will never again put you or anyone else in that position. I will never sign someone else's name like that," she shivered involuntarily as the cold seemed to seep into her coat. "Trust me, that's a lesson I've well-learned."

Ryan was quiet, once again looking out over the city, obviously in thought. Elise's stomach was in turmoil. Would he be able to forgive her? Would his black and white world view prevent him from tolerating any gray?

He turned to her, his eyes open and honest. "Elise Hutchins, I can't fault your heart, your motives, or your character. Your secret is safe with me."

"Thank you, Ryan. That means a lot to me. I appreciate your willingness to revise your initial opinion of me, and I know it probably hasn't been the most fun day ever to follow me around."

Ryan shrugged. "I've enjoyed being your shadow. Although I do wish you hadn't needed to remain inconspicuous at the dance class. It would have been fun to do that with you."

Elise was surprised, and her mind immediately set to spinning. Maybe Ryan would want to come to the class next week. Maybe she should also invite Britney and... no. She needed to give up on that angle. Besides, Ryan would be adamantly opposed to being involved in one of her matches, especially if it involved Britney.

"Maybe we could take the class together some other time," Elise offered. "Have you done any dancing before? I've been taking the class for months now, and I like to think I'm progressing past the beginner stage."

"Oh, really?" Ryan asked, the city lights reflecting in a teasing glint in his eyes. "Prove it."

"What do you mean?" Elise asked, a little suspicious of his light-hearted tone.

Slowly, deliberately, Ryan leaned forward. Then he whispered, "Dance with me."

Not waiting for a response, Ryan took her hand and spun her around gently. "We didn't get to dance earlier, so let's make sure we do it now."

Elise laughed as Ryan began twirling her in the steps of a swing dance. Since yesterday, there had been so much tension between them and so much pressure to prove herself. It was so nice to have all that gone now and be free to enjoy a little silliness. Their laughter was the only music as Ryan swung Elise around in an elaborate pattern. She was soon breathless, but she didn't know if it was from the movement, the laughing, or the fact that she was dancing with a handsome man.

"Yes, I would say you're progressing very nicely," he said, twirling her to a sudden halt.

"I had no idea you could dance!" Elise said.

"There's a lot about me you apparently don't know. So you know how to swing, but how about the waltz?"

Before she had time to respond, he swung her into a waltz across the length of the overlook, with the Seattle skyline their backdrop. Instead of the fairy godmother, Elise now felt as if she was Cinderella, wearing a beautiful ball gown and dancing with a handsome prince. But then their laughter faded and she gradually became aware of the feel of Ryan's arms holding her close in the dance. The night was still, yet there was no need for accompaniment. They moved together as if hearing the same music.

Elise felt Ryan's breath on her ear as they swayed slowly across the grass. "You said earlier that I dislike you. You've also said that I doubt your character and think the worst of you. You couldn't be more wrong. The truth is: I like you far too much. And everything I find out about you only makes me care all the more."

What was happening? Elise looked up into Ryan's eyes, finding an expression that seemed almost brooding, mysterious, and full of... desire? At the eye contact, Ryan's movements leading her through the dance slowed to a stop. Elise was close enough to smell the masculine, outdoorsy scent that surrounded him. She was cold everywhere except where his one hand touched her back and his other hand clasped hers.

Ryan pulled her to him, cradling her close in his arms. Like a magnet, Elise felt herself drawn to him. His warm hand reached up, caressing her cheek. "You're so beautiful Elise," he whispered. "Beautiful in every way."

Her heart rate accelerated. Her breath became shallow. Her lips tingled in anticipation. He was going to kiss her.

Chapter 15

Elise stood on her tiptoes. It felt as if tiny shivers coursed through her entire body. She felt his warm breath as he paused right before their lips met.

Britney.

In that instant before contact, the name whispered through her mind as if on a gentle breeze. Elise gently yet firmly pushed on Ryan's chest and stepped back, their lips never having touched.

Ryan let her go.

Elise's delicious shivers of anticipation now turned to great tremors of shock and disappointment. She felt as if something of infinite value had been stolen from her, leaving her bereft.

"I'm sorry," she whispered brokenly. "I can't." She turned and walked away.

She wanted to explain. She *needed* to explain. But at that moment, she wasn't sure if the choking sobs would win or the desire to return to the refuge of Ryan's forbidden arms and try to reclaim what she had just refused. She needed distance.

She didn't go far, simply walking the few yards back to the edge of the overlook. She took great breaths of the cool air, trying to slow her racing heart and soothe her wayward emotions.

Seconds ticked by. Then she felt Ryan come up behind her and put his hands on her shoulders. Gently, he wrapped his arms around her. She could feel his solid frame behind her, and despite her best intentions, she found herself leaning back into his embrace, letting him support and comfort her with his strength.

"Talk to me, Elise," his lips whispered against her hair. "What's wrong?"

"Britney," she answered hoarsely. "I can't have you for myself when my best friend is crazy about you! It would be like stealing you away from her."

"It wouldn't be stealing. I never belonged to her. I've probably not ever had longer than a five minute conversation with her."

"I know you'd like her if you just got to know her better. Britney is a very nice person. I know she can come across as shallow, but there really isn't a more loyal person in the world. And she's a lot more outgoing and adventurous than I am. She's always been the one to push me out of the box I like to hide in." Elise's voice lowered, her tone filled with anguish. "I can't stand the thought of hurting her. I'm not the type to steal another girl's guy."

"I am *not* her guy!" Ryan said with vehemence. "I never have been. I never will be. It doesn't matter how nice she is."

"But she likes you so much!"

"But I don't like her. Not it that way." Ryan released Elise and firmly turned her around to face him. His hands remained at her shoulders as he determinedly captured her eyes with his, making sure he had her full attention.

"It's you I like," he said resolutely. I've liked you from even before yesterday. I've watched you both at church and at the library. My impression of you was always that you were sweet, conscientious, and godly. I'd been wanting to get to know you better. When that book I ordered never showed up, I was secretly glad. That gave me an excuse to talk to you."

"I had no idea you even knew I existed!"

"I think we've already established that you are awful at observing situations concerning yourself," he said with a wry grin. "How could I not know you existed? You walk into a room and light it up. You're very reserved, yet you are always the one helping and working at church. As I mentioned before, I pride myself on being a good judge of character. Part of the reason I got so upset about the whole Britney / flower situation is because I felt like I'd been wrong about you—wrong about the kind of woman you were and wrong about my impressions of you. Now I know I wasn't wrong. I know that you're everything I hoped for and more. And I'm not willing to lose this chance. I'm not interested in Britney or anyone else. Only you."

Elise shut her eyes, battling between the desire to savor his words and the need to focus and keep a clear head. He was saying all the words she'd been waiting her whole life to hear, and yet she could not allow herself to claim them. She understood that Ryan would probably never be interested in Britney, but she also understood that it didn't matter. She still couldn't hurt Britney by starting a relationship with the man her friend longed for. In Elise's mind, Britney's affections for Ryan Jenkins, unrequited though they were, made the man forever off-limits to Elise.

"I'm sorry," she whispered through the tears coursing down her face. "I wish I could... but I can't."

Ryan was quiet. Elise felt him studying her for a long moment, but she couldn't return his gaze. She felt a physical, searing pain in her chest as if her heart was breaking in two.

"Okay," Ryan said finally.

Surprised at his acceptance, Elise's gaze shot to his face, expecting to find sarcasm or anger. Instead, she found only gentleness, compassion, and maybe even respect, but there was also sadness.

"Elise, I can't fault you for character traits that I find so attractive. If your loyalty, integrity, and your determination make it impossible for you to even give us a chance, then I can't and won't ask you to violate those. Those are some of the very reasons I like you so much." As he spoke, he gently wiped each of her tears with his own fingers. Then he bent, pressed his forehead to hers, and closed his eyes. She knew he longed to kiss her. She still felt the invisible bands of attraction binding them together.

After a long moment, he gently pressed a kiss to her forehead and released her. "Let's get you home before I lose the little restraint I have left," he said, hurrying with her back across the grass to her car.

After Ryan helped her into the car, Elise watched as he crossed the street, turned back, and waved goodbye. Elise pulled the car into the street. She fought back the tears that burned the back of her throat. If she could just make it home, her pillow would be waiting to muffle her sobs and catch her tears in Ryan's absence.

Chapter 16

Elise looked at the clock for the tenth time in the past five minutes. She didn't like confrontation, but this couldn't be avoided. If she waited any longer, Britney would be gone. Though she'd wanted to talk to her friend immediately when Elise had arrived at work, she had patiently waited until she knew Britney's shift ended. Now Elise officially went on break and headed to the staff area where she knew Britney would be.

Knowing she needed to talk to her friend in person, Elise had purposely not called Britney on the phone. She also hadn't trusted herself to handle it well before now. Elise didn't normally anger easily, but even after all this time, she was still having difficulty controlling her feelings toward her friend.

Elise stopped before turning the corner to the hallway leading to the staff room, silently praying that God would help her to be calm and give her the words to say what was needed.

Elise took a deep breath, turned the corner, and stopped. Her mouth dropped open. Standing in the hallway in front of her was Britney. She was in her coat, obviously ready to leave, and giving Oliver Purdue one award-winning goodbye kiss.

Britney giggled as the kiss ended. "I guess I'll see you later," she said.

"With more of that to look forward to, you'll definitely see me later," Oliver answered.

Turning, Britney saw Elise standing at the entrance to the hallway and stopped. "Oh… hi, Elise. I was just coming to find you."

Yeah, right! Elise thought. It was much more likely Britney had been intending on sneaking out without a word

"Britney, we need to talk," Elise said, finding her voice.

"I have to get back to work," Oliver interrupted, having the decency to blush crimson at Elise's presence. "I'll see you two later."

Without waiting for Britney to respond, Elise marched forward, grabbed her friend by the arm, and pulled her into the staff break room. Thankfully, the room was empty. Elise turned to face Britney. She wasn't planning on leaving until Britney had done a whole lot of explaining.

"What is going on?" Elise demanded fiercely.

"You mean with Oliver? I guess we're kind of together now. Why are you looking at me like that? You've been trying to convince me to date Oliver for a long time. Now I am, and you're looking at me like I'm a villain!"

"I know you, Britney. I'm not fully convinced you aren't a villain!" It would be just like Britney to be dating Oliver due to some ulterior motive. Maybe she found out he'd just come in possession of some large inheritance. Maybe she needed him to do something for her. Maybe someone had dared her to go out with him. The list of possibilities was endless, and not one of the scenarios whipping through Elise's head painted Britney in a favorable light.

"What made you change your mind?" Elise demanded, folding her arms across her front.

A little smile lifted the corners of Britney's lips. "A couple nights ago, when you went to see your play, I got called to come back into work because someone was sick. Oliver was working too. After the library closed and we got off, he insisted on walking me to my car. You know he doesn't like me to walk alone that late at night."

"Yeah, he's walked me to my car a few times too," Elise acknowledged.

"Anyway, when we got to my car, it wouldn't start. I was really upset. I'd just had the thing in the shop for maintenance, and the mechanics had given it a clean bill of health. Did you know that Oliver is like a genius when it comes to cars? Before I knew it, he had the hood up, and about three minutes later, the car was running. Apparently, he and his dad have restored a bunch of old cars. Oliver's pretty crazy about anything with wheels. Here I thought he was just a geeky computer nerd.

Britney paused to sigh happily, seeming to savor the memory. "I was so relieved and thankful to him for fixing my car that I offered to buy him dinner sometime. Instead, he suggested that we go out for coffee right then. We got to talking, and one thing led to another. Next thing I know, we had talked until 3:00 in the morning! Then yesterday, we worked the same shift and spent the entire evening together. I think it was the best Valentine's Day I've ever had!"

"I thought you weren't even attracted to Oliver," Elise said, still a little skeptical. She was almost afraid to hope that things would work well out for her friend.

"I didn't think I was. But I didn't know him before. I guess I was so busy trying to get him to leave me alone that I didn't even take the time to get to know him. Everything was based on a first impression of him being a nerd who was way too young. But now I know how interesting, sweet, and romantic he is. He's so smart, but he's a lot of fun too. I don't know that I have ever felt this way before. Aren't you happy for me, Elise? You should be thrilled. You're the one who's tried to push me to get together with him. You've always been his biggest cheerleader. I'm surprised you never tried to... wait a minute. Elise Hutchins, did you set me up? Did you sabotage my car just so Oliver would have to fix it for me?"

Elise burst out laughing, ending the tension that had held the room captive. "No! I promise, Britney. I had absolutely nothing to do with that one. I don't set up close friends. I am as surprised as you are. I didn't even know Oliver had any car experience. I guess sometimes God handles His own matchmaking."

Britney beamed. "I really like him, Elise. I guess I should have listened to you... about everything." A shadow crossed her face, and she looked troubled. Then, with an uncharacteristic look of determination and a straightening of her spine,

Britney looked directly at Elise. "I have a confession to make."

Then, with a deep breath, she spoke in a rush. "I used your florist account to send flowers to myself. I had the card signed with Ryan's name. I thought if I pretended they were from him and thanked him, he would be too embarrassed to deny it. It worked for Chandra and Damon. I thought it might work for me too."

"Britney, I—"

"Please don't interrupt me, Elise. This is hard enough as it is. If you say something now, I may never get this all out."

Elise obediently shut her mouth, and Britney, looking thoroughly miserable, continued. "Remember when I went with you to choose flowers for that lady from your church who was in the hospital? That's how I knew the floral shop where you had an account. So I called them and pretended I was you. They didn't even question me when I asked to have it added to my, or your, account. Then when the roses were delivered, I pretended to be surprised. When Ryan came into the library, I showed him the flowers and thanked him profusely. But it didn't work. He said he didn't send them and asked to see the card. Then he seemed upset and almost angry, still denying that he sent them. It was completely humiliating, and I'm so very sorry. I should have listened to you, and I was stupid for ever doing something like that. Can you please forgive me?"

"Britney, I already knew what you'd done."

"How did you know? Did the florist call you?"

"No, Ryan told me. He thought I was the one who'd sent the flowers and signed his name. Unfortunately, I'm the one he blamed."

"What do you mean Ryan told you? When? I talked to him just this morning to apologize, and I confessed the entire thing to him. He knows you weren't involved."

"You talked to him this morning?" Elise asked, shocked. "When? How? What did you say?"

"He came into the library before your shift started. I felt I had to make things right, so I told him that I was the one who sent the flowers. I even explained that I did it because I'd wanted him to like me."

"But he already knows it was my account, Britney!" Elise tried to explain. "He checked with the florist two days ago. Now he probably just thinks you're trying to cover for me!"

"No!" Britney denied with wide eyes. "I told him I used your account. He asked me if you had anything to do with it, and I said no. I told him you would never do that sort of thing. I mean you're still scarred from when we did that to Chandra, even though that worked out just fine."

"You told him about that?" Elise asked, incredulous. She really didn't want Ryan knowing the details of one of the most shameful moments of her life. He didn't really need to think worse of her.

"Well, yeah," Britney replied defensively. "I didn't know I wasn't supposed to. I explained about Chandra, but I didn't tell him you're Cupid or anything."

"He already knows I'm Cupid!" Elise moaned in exasperation. "He figured it out when he thought I had tried to set the two of you up by sending those flowers."

"Well, that explains why he was looking for you and carrying around that newspaper. He was probably wanting to show you the article."

"What newspaper? What article?"

"You haven't seen it yet?" Britney looked around the room and then grabbed a newspaper from the large table in the center of the small break room. "Here," she said, shoving it into Elise's face and pointing to an article.

The article was titled, "Love Letters to Seattle's Cupid." As Elise quickly read it, she couldn't help the smile that spread across her face. It was all about the new hype surrounding this mysterious Cupid who was setting up love matches around the city. It was amusing to her that she'd had nothing to do with some of the many matches attributed to Cupid. But Elise realized Seattle's Cupid was fast becoming an urban legend; at which point, the truth was a lot less important than the romance of the story.

The article also talked about how so many people were now wishing and longing for Seattle's Cupid to choose them for a match. Two letters for Cupid were printed beside the article. The letters were written by two different women who each detailed the sad story of her love life and concluded with a plea that Cupid find a match for her.

Elise was completely delighted. After all, there was not one single criticism of Cupid or *his* methods in the article. Everyone was wanting a love match courtesy of Cupid.

"Ryan saw this?" she asked.

"I think so. He came to the library looking for you. I recognized this newspaper as the one he was holding. If he really thought you were the one who'd sent the flowers falsely, he sure didn't seem upset with you. In fact, I might even think that he liked you."

"And would you be okay with that?" Elise asked cautiously. "Would you be okay if Ryan liked someone else? And if that someone else was me?"

Britney squealed and threw her arms around Elise. "So he does like you! Why wouldn't I be okay with it? I don't know that I ever liked Ryan as much as I liked the idea of Ryan. Handsome lawyer, successful... But now I have Oliver. As humiliating as it was to confess, I couldn't take the guilt of what I'd done, especially since Oliver and I are together now. I told Ryan about Oliver and explained that now I just wanted to make things right with him for trying to trick him and with you for using your account."

Britney paused, her expression returning to troubled. "So what do you think? I know it was awful, but can you forgive me?"

Elise smiled. "Yes, I can forgive you. You know I've never been good at staying angry with you, even when you deserve it. And you very much deserve it this time, especially since I was the one who Ryan blamed for the whole deception. He thought I was an awful person!"

"But why didn't you tell him it wasn't you? It shouldn't have taken you much to figure out it was me. You should have just told him!"

"I knew it was you alright. But I couldn't incriminate you like that. You liked him; I didn't want him thinking badly of you. Besides, he was so angry, he wouldn't have believed me anyway."

"Thank you, Elise." Britney's eyes looked suspiciously red beneath heavily mascaraed lashes. "You know I don't deserve your loyalty. Hopefully I've at least fixed things so he knows I'm the one to blame."

"I appreciate you taking responsibility and admitting what you did," Elise said genuinely. "I know it couldn't have been easy. How did Ryan take it? Did he say anything else?"

Britney shrugged. "He didn't say much. He seemed surprised and a bit upset, but I'm not sure why. He did ask a strange question as he was leaving though."

"Oh, really? What was it?"

"He asked if you'd ever been up in the Space Needle."

Chapter 17

"Have a nice night, Sheila"

"You too, Elise."

Sheila went out the door while Elise turned to punch in the code to set the library's security system.

It was late. The library had closed at 10:00, and Elise was the last one to leave. With the security system set, Elise walked out the door and let it fall locked behind her. It was a dark night with clouds covering the moon, but at least it wasn't raining. Elise started down the steps, reluctantly leaving the exterior lights of the library behind.

Strangely, Sheila was standing at the bottom of the steps, as if waiting for Elise.

"Is something wrong, Sheila?" Elise asked as she approached. "Did you want to walk together?"

"I was told to give this to you," Sheila said, smiling mysteriously as she extended a white envelope.

"By who?" Elise took the envelope and automatically began opening it.

Sheila remained silent, but her open excitement and curiosity spoke volumes as she peered over Elise's shoulder.

Elise took out two small pieces of paper. One looked like some kind of ticket. The other was a plain white sheet. Turning toward the lights from the library, Elise tried to identify the ticket. At the words "Space Needle," Elise's heart took off in a sprint. Angling the other paper to see more clearly, she found the words, "I will be waiting."

"Sheila, who... ? What... ?

But she already knew who.

Sheila laughed. "You'd better hurry," she said, having obviously gotten a good view of the papers. "I wouldn't keep a man who looked like he did waiting very long."

Elise laughed. "Thanks, Sheila." And before she wasted more time trying to analyze the "what ifs," she took off sprinting.

"I expect a full report!" Sheila called.

Elise's thoughts caught up with her during the drive. What if it wasn't who she thought it was? The

Space Needle would be closed by now. What was she supposed to do once she got there? Had she misunderstood? Maybe the ticket was for a specific time tomorrow and not for her to use immediately. And then, the worst thought of all: What if someone was just toying with her, trying to give her a little taste of her own medicine?

Elise's steps gradually slowed as she walked from her car to Seattle's iconic monument. This was ridiculous. She must have just misunderstood.

A man stood outside the door.

Elise hesitantly approached, nervously fingering the ticket in her hand. "I... um... was supposed to come..."

"You must be Elise Hutchins," the man said with a smile. "Right this way, miss. We've been expecting you."

The man escorted her to the elevator and even pushed the button for the observation deck. "Enjoy your time," he said with a smile and a wave as the elevator doors shut.

Elise's heart pounded so furiously that she couldn't take a deep breath. She closed her eyes, trying to relax as the elevator ascended. She really didn't want to ruin everything by hyperventilating or passing out.

The doors opened onto the empty observation deck. Elise cautiously stepped out, scanning the entire area. But it appeared as if it was completely deserted. Not knowing what to do, Elise walked over to the large windows fronting the circumference of the deck. Her breath caught. Seattle was lit up like a Christmas tree, each beautiful spark winking up at her. As she slowly walked around, she could almost imagine she was flying over the city.

But what was most spectacular was the silence. She was completely alone. Seeing such beauty in utter quiet and knowing that all the lights below represented thousands of people living their lives created an experience that was both exquisite and profound.

A voice finally broke the stillness. "Miss Hutchins?"

Elise turned to find a man dressed in what looked like a waiter's attire and holding a vase of lovely red roses.

"These flowers are for you."

As soon as Elise reached out and accepted the flowers, the man turned and left, disappearing back in the direction of the elevator.

In amongst the flowers, a small envelope stood at attention. Elise carefully extracted the card from its case. She turned it over, looking at both the front and back in confusion. It was blank.

"Those are from me," a deep voice said.

Elise's gaze shot up, meeting Ryan's smiling face and twinkling eyes. He walked toward her. Reaching out, he gently took the blank card from her fingers. Then he took out a pen from his jacket pocket. After writing on the card, he handed it back to Elise.

"I didn't want there to be any doubt that I signed it myself," he said with a smile.

Elise looked at the card. It very clearly had the words, 'To, Elise. From, Ryan Jenkins.'

"Why... ? How did you arrange all this?" Elise said, gesturing to include the flowers and everything around them.

"Well, I did get some matchmaking tips from observing the best, but I also called in a few favors for the logistics. The restaurant is officially closed like everything else, but I have also arranged for a private, late-night dinner there whenever we're ready. As to why..."

Ryan took the vase from Elise and set it on the floor. Then he took both her hands in his, a. Making sure he had her full attention, he spoke. "I know you already said we couldn't be together, but considering the new developments with Britney, I'm hoping to change your mind. I was completely wrong about you. You have more character, more heart, and more integrity than any woman I've ever met. You should have told me you didn't send the flowers. I behaved terribly to you and said all-manner of awful things, judging your morals and conviction. But you went through all of that and took the full blame in order to protect your friend. I am so sorry for wrongfully judging you.

Before Elise could respond to his apology, he spoke again. "I have no words to describe how much I respect and admire your loyalty toward both Britney and what you see as your calling. You're right; you help people. Whatever tools you use to create a matchmaking scenario are obviously well thought-out, prayed about, and ultimately desired by those involved. Everyone wants to be deceived if it results in the potential to fall in love.

Ryan hesitated, his smile turning adoably sheepish before he confessed, "So… I'm new at being a matchmaker, but I thought Cupid needed her own set-up. Elise Hutchins, I'm willing to try any and all methods for even a chance with you."

"You're a little late, you know," Elise said with a smile. "The most romantic day of the year is supposed to be Valentine's Day, and that was yesterday."

"I know. But I'm willing to present a good case in my defense."

"Oh, really," Elise said, raising an eyebrow in an expression of curiosity.

"Yes, just give me 364 days, and I'm sure I can fully convince you to be my valentine."

Elise laughed.

Ryan's teasing gaze turned serious. Elise watched in fascination as his hazel eyes darkened to brown.

"Elise," he whispered, his hands sliding up her arms and drewing her close. Holding one of her hands in his and curling the other around her back, he swung her into a slow waltz. They danced around the entire circular room, gliding over a 360 degree view of Seattle below. The lights of the city twirled through her vision as she spun, but the one constant was Ryan.

Elise looked up, his face mere inches from her own. Their connection was so intense that their dance unconsciously slowed and finally stopped.

"Have you no idea what you've done?" Ryan asked softly. "You have lured me into Cupid's world, struck me with one of your arrows, and brought me under your spell. You now hold me completely mesmerized."

He slowly, gently bent his head, meeting her lips with his. Elise's heart ached as she savored the beauty of the moment. It was just the two of them, alone in the world, high above Seattle's skyline. He held her like she'd always dreamed of being held, and kissed her like she'd never dared to dream. His kiss was a long, gentle caress but with an ever-building passion beneath the surface. She was sure she would never breathe again, and wasn't sure if she wanted to.

Finally, his lips released hers, separating only a few inches while he continued to hold her close.

"So, what's your ruling, Cupid? Will you at least give me a chance to present my case?"

Elise smiled, stood on her tiptoes, and lightly brushed a kiss on his lips. "Ryan, feel free to practice any of your future matchmaking schemes on me, and I can pretend to take a long time deliberating a verdict. But the truth is, I think you already won the case with your opening argument."

Ryan smiled in pure delight and pulled her close in another breathtaking kiss.

And with that, Cupid made her match.

Author's Note

Time for my confession.

As with many of my books, *The Random Acts of Cupid* has a kernel of truth. When I was in high school, my friends and I took turns playing practical jokes on each other as birthday "gifts." Yes, I did receive lacy panties in Art class. And yes, I did take part in sending one of my best friends flowers signed with the name of the boy she liked. And, worst of all, yes, she did thank him before I had a chance to tell her the truth.

Unfortunately, that's where the truth in this story ends. Things did not turn out nearly so romantic for my friend, and I have never in my life attempted matchmaking. Thankfully, there were no lasting effects from my poorly executed joke. My friend quickly forgave me and went on to be my roommate in college. She remains one of my best friends today.

And don't worry, she got her revenge. I think sending me a letter from a rather notorious magazine requesting my modeling services was payment enough, especially when that letter was delivered in English class and passed around to every other student before I got to see it.

Have you ever done something that, even years later, causes you to cringe in embarrassment at the memory? This is one of those experiences for me.

I've heard it said that nothing bad ever happens to a writer, it's all just material. While reliving the vivid memory of this experience, my imagination got to turning, thinking... what if it had turned out well? Thus, the idea for this book was born.

Now that I have completed my humiliation by confessing to all of you, I would also like to include a reminder. At the time, I wanted to bury my head in the sand and pretend I had never, even inadvertently, done something so shameful. Little did I know that God would be able to use that bad experience as fodder for me to write this book. You see, I don't think it's just authors. If you're letting God have it all, even you at your absolute worst, then it's all just material in His hands.

> *"And we know that for those who love God all things work together for good, for those who are called according to his purpose."*
> *Romans 8:28*

Other books by Amanda Tru

YESTERDAY series:
Yesterday
The Locket
Today
The Choice
Tomorrow
The Promise

TRU EXCEPTIONS series:
Baggage Claim
Mirage
Point of Origin

Christian Romance:
Secret Santa
The Random Acts of Cupid
The Assumption of Guilt

Romance
The Romance of the Sugar Plum Fairy

Please continue reading

Sneak Peek of…

Yesterday

A Christian Romantic Suspense/Time Travel Romance

Book 1

Chapter 1

Red flashed against the bright white of the snow.

I slammed on the brakes. The SUV skidded toward the guardrail.

My heart seemed to stop. I couldn't breathe. My body felt suspended as the mountainous terrain whirled across my vision. I braced for impact. Unexpectedly, the vehicle lurched as the tires found traction and came to a sudden stop

I sucked in air. My eyes frantically searched the heavy snowfall.

What had I seen?

Was it human?

Had I hit something?

The Sierra mountains were shrouded in the stillness of the winter storm, silent and revealing no secrets. Had I just imagined something dart in front of me?

I caught a glimpse of a fist out of the corner of my eye. I jumped. A strangled scream escaped my throat as the fist started hammering on my window. Heart thumping, I peered beyond the relentless pounding to see the outline of a woman in a red parka. She was screaming, but I couldn't understand her words.

Fingers fumbling and shaking, I rolled down my window. At her appearance, an electric current of shock ripped through me.

Blood streamed from somewhere on her head. It trickled down to her chin, leaving a dark red trail. Dirty tears streaked her cheeks, and her hair hung in clumps of frizzy knots.

I frantically jerked open my door.

"Are you okay?" I asked.

But she didn't answer. Instead, she continued to scream, her hysterical cries now slicing through me.

"Help! Help! Please help me! I can't get them out!"

What was she talking about? My eyes traced an invisible line to where she was gesturing. A few yards in front of my own fender, the meager guardrail was bent and scraped. Peering through the falling snow, I could see beyond that to where the frozen earth had been torn up. Standing on the frame of my car door, I looked into the embankment off the side. Red tail lights glowed like beacons.

The shock to my senses was like a physical blow. I sprang out of the car, stepping into a blood stained patch of snow. Blood had dripped from the woman's leg where her torn pants exposed a jagged wound. Her sobbing and frantic cries continued, but she wasn't making sense.

Her skin was chalky green. She was in shock, yet I felt paralyzed. My medical background consisted of a three hour CPR and first aid class I'd taken over a year ago. Panic washed over me like a wave. I didn't know how to help her!

Desperate, I gently pushed her toward the back seat of the SUV. Her feet shuffled forward two steps, and then she collapsed. I caught her around the shoulders and practically dragged her rag doll frame.

She roused enough to help as I lifted her into the back seat. I unraveled the scarf from my neck and wrapped it around her leg above the bloody gash, tying it as tightly as I could.

Reaching into the back of the SUV, I located a large flashlight and my old coat that I used when skiing. I wrapped the arms of the coat loosely around her leg, hoping the bulky material would soak up some of the blood.

"What's your name?" I asked the woman.

She cleared her throat and shook her head, her brow creasing with confusion. Instead, she began a new litany of faint but frantic cries about her family.

"You can tell me later. I'm Hannah."

"Help! My family . . . !"

"I'm going down into the ravine right now. Stay here. I'll help them. I promise."

Hoping I didn't just make a promise I couldn't keep, I shut the door and tripped my way through the snowdrifts toward the red haloed taillights.

I pulled my phone out of my coat pocket. There usually wasn't cell phone coverage on this road. But, just maybe . . .

No service.

This wasn't supposed to be happening! I should be at my sister's lodge at the top of the mountain not crawling down a steep embankment to help accident victims!

It wasn't even supposed to be snowing! I'd checked the weather report at least a dozen times: no new snow for the next week. Now it was practically a blizzard!

I took deep breaths, trying to control the panic and adrenaline running through my veins as I half climbed, half slid down the incline. This wasn't me. I'm not the brave sort. In fact, I'm pretty much a wimp!

I was facing the risk of a serious panic attack even before any of this had happened. The rational part of my brain said my fear was ridiculous. The roads were supposed to be clear. I'd driven to Silver Springs many times before. And, I was driving the biggest, meanest, previously-owned SUV an over-protective father could buy for his college-age daughter. Despite my best rationale, my hands were sweating, my heart was beating erratically, and I was still at the bottom of the mountain.

But those symptoms were nothing compared to what I experienced now. When my eyes collided with the blue sedan at the bottom, I wanted to turn around and run. The front of the car was wrapped around a tree. How could anyone survive an accident like this?

The gas station attendant's ramblings from earlier replayed in my head like a bad movie. Something about a tragic accident on this same road five years ago. The family had all died.

Taking a deep breath, I felt renewed determination run through my veins as it hitched a ride on an abundance of adrenaline. I had to do this.

"Hello, can anyone hear me?" I called as I slid the last few feet to the bottom of the ravine. My wrist scraped over some exposed branches on the way down, but the pain didn't register. I called again, louder.

No answer.

I didn't want to do this! I didn't want to see the scene inside the mangled car. I drew in a shaky, hiccuping breath.

Reaching the driver's side door, I shined the flashlight inside. The beam flickered in my shaking hand. I counted three passengers, motionless and unresponsive to the bright light. My stomach flipped as the beam caught blood marring each pale face.

I bent over, hyperventilating and gasping for breath. I couldn't do this! They were probably already dead! I closed my eyes. "Please, God, I can't do this! Help me!"

I released my breath slowly, then quickly swung my flashlight back inside before I lost my nerve.

The driver must be the injured woman's husband. In the back seat were two children. The girl I guessed to be about 7; the boy about 5. Though I put all my weight into it, neither door on the driver's side would budge.

I rushed around to the other side, climbing into the mom's empty seat. Reaching into the back seat and searching for the girl's pulse, I sighed in relief. She was alive—unconscious, but with a strong pulse. I climbed further over the seats and reached for the boy. Another pulse! New energy and determination surged through my veins.

Finally, I leaned over to the dad for a pulse. But I already knew the answer. The front driver's side had taken most of the impact. No one could survive in his position. To my surprise, I felt a slight bump against my finger. It was very faint, but the man was alive . . . at least for now.

I tried to focus. What could I do? I could drive to the lodge and get my sister, Abby, and her husband, Tom, to come help. We could use the phone at the lodge to call for medical assistance. Then we could get some of the other lodgers, come back and . . .

I shivered, feeling the freezing cold seep through my coat. It would be too late. I closed my eyes. A sob of fear and frustration caught in my throat. We wouldn't make it back in time. They couldn't survive their injuries or these temperatures for very long. I couldn't leave them. It was all up to me.

I tried not to think. I tried not to feel. I just acted.

The door by the girl opened easily. I unbuckled her seatbelt, took a deep breath, and hoisted her in my arms. She stirred and moaned slightly.

"I've got you. You're going to be alright," I cooed softly as I struggled through the drifts and still-falling snow back up the ravine.

My arms burned with the effort and my labored breathing came in short gasps. Just when I thought I couldn't take another step, I finally reached the SUV. Gently, I placed the girl in the back seat beside her mother.

"Maddie! "The sobbing woman gathered her daughter into her arms.

"I think she's going to be okay," I said, shocked the woman was still conscious. "I have to go back for the others."

Knowing every minute counted, I hurried back to the ravine and climbed into the back seat of the car. I unbuckled the boy's seat belt. He stirred and groaned, his eyes fluttering open.

"Hi, I'm Hannah. I'm going to get you out of here. Where are you hurt?"

"My legs and my head."

The driver's seat was pushed up against him. We both had to work to free his pinned legs. Grunting and groaning, I eventually dragged him out.

Even though this was my second trip back up the ravine, the boy was much easier to carry. Because he was conscious, he wasn't the dead weight his sister had been. As he held on to my neck and buried his face in my hair, I learned his name was Timmy and his favorite thing was fire trucks.

When I put Timmy in the back seat of the SUV, I saw that his mom was struggling to remain conscious.

I faced a moment of indecision. The man might already be dead. It had been tough carrying the kids, and I had no idea how I was going to get a large man up the ravine. Besides, if I took the time to get him, it might be too late for the mom.

Hesitating, I realized it wasn't really a decision. I wouldn't be able to live with myself if I didn't at least try. Having a sudden epiphany, I opened the back of my SUV and removed a tow rope and a tarp.

Since I'd always had a healthy fear of just about every worst case scenario, I took seriously the motto, "Always be prepared." My phobias insured I had well-stocked emergency supplies. I'd just never imagined this situation was one I'd need to prepare for.

When I got to the sedan, I found the man's pulse still barely registering life. It was probably good he was unconscious. He was stuck. I pushed and pulled, trying not to think about any other pain or injuries I may be inflicting. I had to get him out.

He wasn't budging even a little. Panting and sweating, I tried to catch my breath. But it kept coming in short gasps.

I couldn't do it! Great sobs scraped past my throat. I was losing it!

"Please help me!" I prayed desperately, yelling at the top of my lungs.

I crawled over him, kicking and punching his seat like a madwoman.

To my shock, the seat broke. I quickly removed the seat back, using the space to pull the man from behind. His lifeless body finally slid from its cage.

Breathing heavily, I dragged him out of the car and onto the tarp I had positioned. I wrapped the tarp around him and tied one end of the rope under his arms. Grabbing the other end, I pulled. The tarp slid across the snow.

Even with the tarp, the man was dead weight. I'd heard that adrenaline had been known to give a person superhuman strength. That and some divine assistance is the only explanation I have for how my 5'6'' frame was able to drag that man uphill out of the ravine and then lift him into the rear of the SUV.

Finally back inside my SUV, my frozen fingers gripped the steering wheel in terror as I drove through the snow. The woman was unconscious now. I had to get to the lodge.

Timmy was the only one conscious. He was amazingly calm. We talked about his Christmas list. From Hot Wheels to remote controls, Timmy wanted such variety of cars and trucks that Santa would have his work cut out for him.

My breath caught with relief as I saw the lights of Silver Springs through the swirling snow. Stopping in front of the lodge, I jumped out. Frantic, I yelled, banging my fists on the front door. An elderly man I didn't recognize opened it.

I don't remember what I told him. Everything I said seemed like gibberish in my head, but he apparently understood.

"Go get McAllister!" he called to an older woman near the stairs. He then turned and explained to me that a doctor was vacationing at the lodge.

The older man and two others gently carried each person to the large living room where the doctor known as McAllister was putting on a pair of rubber gloves.

Scanning the patients, he called to the man from the door. "George, we're going to need a helicopter."

My eyes met the doctor's blue-green ones and held. He was a lot younger than I had expected, with a strong face and dark, wavy blond hair to go with those rather incredible eyes.

"Who's injured the worst?" he asked.

"The man," I replied. "I'm not sure he's still alive. His pulse was very weak even before I pulled him out of the wreck."

Dr. McAllister's eyes shot back to me, sizing me up. Obviously having questions, he said instead, "I need some help."

Maybe he assumed I had some medical training. Then again, maybe I was just the best choice of assistants. The other three guys in the room didn't look like they would be able to tell the difference between a pair of tweezers and a chainsaw.

I followed Dr. McAllister as he checked each patient. I don't remember what he did. I was in a daze, simply following his orders.

The loud chopping of a helicopter broke the hush of the room. Paramedics rushed in with gurneys and quickly transferred the family to the waiting helicopter. As the lights and sounds faded away, Dr. McAlister took my hand, led me to a couch in front of the fire, and placed a mug of hot cocoa in my stiff fingers.

He sat down beside me, his gaze concerned. "I haven't even asked if you are hurt."

"No. Just cold."

He wrapped a blanket around me, saying, "Can you tell me what happened?"

Almost like a recitation, I recounted every detail, but it was like I was talking about someone else. I felt nothing.

When I finished, I asked softly, "Are they going to be alright, Dr. McAlister?" I vaguely noticed that my hands around the mug had begun shaking.

He winced. Seeing my cocoa was about to slosh out of my hands, he took the mug, put it on the coffee table, and held my cold hands in his warm ones.

His eyes met mine. "Call me Seth. And I'm not really a doctor, not yet anyway. I'm in medical school. George is an old friend who tends to exaggerate my accomplishments and ignore my faults."

"I'm Hannah."

Knowing I was still waiting for an answer, he sighed. "I think the kids are going to be fine. I'm not sure about the mom. She's lost a lot of blood. I don't think the dad will make it. They'll do everything possible, but his chances are very slim."

I appreciated his honesty. "I don't know why my hands are shaking," I murmured. Thinking back to what I had done, I felt a burning behind my eyes. "I had to do a lot of maneuvering to get the man out of the car. It was really rough. Maybe I hurt him more."

I whispered. "Do you think he'll die because of something I did?"

Warm tears rolled down my face. Seth took my face in his gentle hands, lifting my chin so our eyes met.

"Hannah, none of those people would have made it without you. Do you understand? They would have all died. You told me, but I still don't understand how you did it. I do know that you saved them." His thumb massaged my cheek. "I don't think I've ever met a woman who was so strong and brave."

I let out an almost hysterical giggle. "I'm not brave at all. If you only knew. My own shadow scares me regularly!"

"You did what had to be done even though you were afraid. I call that bravery."

Seeing his honest face looking at me with such admiration, I lost it. The shaking hands turned into full body convulsions. The hysterical giggling transformed into heaving sobs. I couldn't catch my breath. My throat, eyes, and chest burned, but I was so cold. I relived yet again every last detail of the night. But this time, I felt everything.

Seth held me close, caressing my hair, wiping my tears, whispering words of comfort. His lips traced gentle kisses across my forehead. While this would normally be a strange intimacy with someone I just met, with Seth it felt right. Comforting.

Eventually I felt the warmth of his strong arms seep through the cold. My sobs lessened as my body relaxed. I clung to Seth. I felt a blessed numbness as warmth stole over me. My eyelids grew impossibly heavy.

As if in a dream, I felt myself being carried, floating up the stairs until I was laid gently upon a soft bed. Seth covered me with a blanket. I tried to speak, but I couldn't remember any words. I felt a gentle kiss on my forehead and a whispered, "Good night." My last memory was of those blue-green eyes and a feather-light touch on my face.

If you enjoyed this preview, POINT OF ORIGIN, and other books by Amanda Tru may be purchased from the same online store where you purchased this book. Happy reading!

About the Author

Amanda loves to write exciting books with plenty of unexpected twists. She figures she loses so much sleep writing the things, it's only fair she makes readers lose sleep with books they can't put down!

Amanda has always loved reading, and writing books has been a lifelong dream. A vivid imagination helps her write captivating stories in a wide variety of genres. Her current book list includes everything from holiday romances, to action-packed suspense, to a Christian time travel / romance series.

Amanda is a former elementary school teacher who now spends her days being mommy to three little boys and her nights furiously writing. Amanda and her family live in a small Idaho town where the number of cows outnumbers the number of people.

You can find Amanda Tru on Facebook or at her website! She loves hearing from readers!

Facebook:
https://www.facebook.com/amandatru.author
Website:
http://www.amandatru.blogspot.com
Email:
truamanda@gmail.com

www.ingramcontent.com/pod-product-compliance
Lightning Source LLC
Chambersburg PA
CBHW071247130626
46556CB00003B/1197